justified lies

tfh team bravo
book three

Melissa Schroeder

For all of the TFH groupies. Thank you always for loving this crew as much as I do.

also by melissa schroeder

THE HARMLESS WORLD

The Original Harmless Five

- A Little Harmless Sex
- A Little Harmless Pleasure
- A Little Harmless Obsession
- A Little Harmless Lie
- A Little Harmless Addiction

Rough 'n Ready

- Rough Submission
- Rough Fascination
- Rough Fantasy
- Rough Ride

Harmless Trouble

- Harmless Secrets
- Harmless Revenge
- Harmless Scandals

The Wulf Family

- Faith
- Taboo
- Trust

A Little Harmless Military Romance

- Infatuation
- Possession
- Surrender

Task Force Hawaii

- Seductive Reasoning
- Hostile Desires
- Constant Craving
- Tangled Passions
- Wicked Temptations
- Twisted Emotions

TFH Team Bravo

- Justified Secrets
- Justified Fear
- Justified Lies
- Justified Revenge (coming soon)

Dillon Security

- Burned

THE CAMOS AND CUPCAKES WORLD

Camos and Cupcakes

- Delicious
- Luscious
- Scrumptious

The Fillmore Siblings

- Hate to Love You
- Love to Hate You

Juniper Springs

- Wild Love
- Crazy Love
- Last Love
- Imperfect Love

THE SANTINI WORLD

The Santinis

- Leonardo
- Marco
- Gianni
- Vicente
- A Santini Christmas
- A Santini in Love
- Falling for a Santini
- One Night with a Santini
- A Santini Takes the Fall
- A Santini's Heart
- Loving a Santini

Semper Fi Marines

- Tease Me
- Tempt Me

- Touch Me

The Fitzpatricks

- Chances Are

THE MELISSA SCHROEDER INSTALOVE COLLECTION

Dominion Rockstar Romance

- Undeniable
- Unpredictable
- Unexpected
- Tempted

Mafia Sisters

- Stealing Destiny
- Guarding Fable

Faking It

- Faking it with my Billionaire Boss
- Faking it with my Brother's Best Friend
- Faking it with my Frenemy

The Fighting Sullivans

- Falling for the General's Daughter
- Falling for the Girl Next Door
- Falling for my Best Friend
- Falling for my Baby Mama

Also Included

- Kiss my Tinsel
- Dad Bod Rockstar

Texas Temptations

- Conquering India
- Delilah's Downfall

Hawaiian Holidays

- Mele Kalikimaka, Baby
- Sex on the Beach
- Getting Lei'd

Once Upon an Accident

- The Accidental Countess
- Lessons in Seduction
- The Spy Who Loved Her

The Cursed Clan

- Callum
- Angus
- Logan
- Fletcher
- Anice

The Sweet Shoppe

- Tempting Prudence
- Cowboy Up
- Her Wicked Warrior

By Blood

- Desire by Blood
- Seduction by Blood

Hands On

- The Hired Hand
- Hands on Training

Telepathic Cravings

- Voices Carry
- Lost in Emotion
- Hard Habit to Break

Bounty Hunters, Inc

- For Love or Honor
- Sinner's Delight

Saints and Sinners

- Seducing the Saint
- Hunting Mila

Lonestar Wolf Pack

- Primal Instincts

Texas Heat

- Scorched

Spies, Lies, and Alibis

- The Boss

SINGLE TITLES

- A Calculated Seduction
- Chasing Luck
- Going for Eight
- Grace Under Pressure
- Operation Love
- Saving Thea
- Snowbound Seduction
- Sweet Patience
- The Last Detail
- The Seduction of Widow McEwan

hawaiian terms

Aloha - Hello, goodbye, love
Bra-Bro
Bruddah- brother, term of endearment
Haole-Newcomer to the islands
Howzit - How is it going?
Kamaʻāina-Local to the islands
Mahalo-Thank you
Malasadas- A Portuguese donut without a hole which started out as a tradition for Shrove (Fat) Tuesday. They are deep fried, dipped in sugar or cinnamon and sugar. In other words, it is a decadent treat every person must try when they go to Hawaii. If you do not try it, you fail. Do yourself a favor. Go to Leonard's and buy one. You are welcome.
Pupule - crazy
Slippahs - slippers, AKA sandals

writing soundtrack

Most of my books have writing soundtracks. They are either songs that inspired the characters or scenes. Some of them played while I plotted the book.

I wanted to note that the dark moment in the book was inspired while I wrote the previous book, Justified Fear. I had *Obliviate* from one of the *Harry Potter* soundtracks. The moment I heard the music the first time, the scene of Eden and Kap's dark moment hit me. I listened to it over and over while I wrote the book.

You can check the rest out on the JUSTIFIED LIES book page on my website.

one

KAPONE HANSON HATED anyone who arrived late. His mama had taught him the importance of showing up on time. She had been married to an Army man, and she had taught school. She was a bit of a tyrant. So, even at the age of thirty-five, he broke out in hives when he was late.

Like right now. He rushed into the TFH headquarters, irritation running up and down his spine. He understood it was insane. It didn't, however, make it any easier to deal with being fifteen minutes late to a job where he didn't have to be on time. Team Bravo's captain was laid back.

The moment he rushed into the common room, the energy was off. Robbie Ramirez, better known as Rami, and Nikki Kekoa were huddled together. For once, they weren't fighting. When Robbie Ramirez looked up at him, he shook his head.

"They've been looking for you, Kap."

"I'm fifteen minutes late," he said, exasperated.

He rolled his eyes. "Not that. You know they don't bust our balls about that."

Since the two active teams were always considered on call, they got a lot of leeway in their schedules.

"Then what?"

"Jesus, Rami," Nikki said, rolling her eyes. "It has to do with a case Alpha got last night. Some victim found dead in Haleiwa."

He frowned. Bravo was a search and rescue team. Granted, they often ended up helping with various cases, but their primary focus was searching for missing people. Alpha team handled more prominent cases. Things that involved foreign dignitaries and...*fuck*. Government officials.

In his life before TFH, Kap had been an NCIS agent. He didn't want to deal with the headache that came with that old life.

The door to the commander's office opened.

"Kap, we need you in here," Seth Harrington called out.

The office was entirely made of glass, so he could see Adam Lee, Team Alpha's captain, along with the commander, of course.

He knew there was no way of avoiding this shit, so he strode into the office.

Martin "Del" Delano was sitting behind his desk. The former Army Ranger had been the original commander of what became Team Alpha. At mid-forty, he was still in top shape. The massive Hawaiian sported his signature bald head and was wearing a TFH polo shirt and cargo pants. He still looked like a hard ass. The only thing that softened him was the multitude of pictures featuring his wife and kids surrounding him.

"What's up?" Kap asked.

"We had a case last night, and we thought you might be able to help us," Adam said.

"Sure. Something to do with NCIS?"

Seth and Adam shared a look.

"What?"

Seth sighed. "The guy was former CIA."

His stomach dipped. Of course, that was the reason they'd pulled him in. It was Monday, and *all* Mondays were shitty.

"Is that a fact?"

"Yes," Seth said. "And he worked with Eden Carlyle at one time."

Fuck. Yep, Mondays were always ballbusters.

"I didn't know that part of her life then."

And he didn't. She'd hidden it from him.

You were dating for only a month.

Shut up.

Adam glanced at the big boss and, apparently, both he and Seth were going to let him take over. Kap looked at his boss.

"Listen, we know it is a sore spot, but, apparently, this Andrew Green was working in the same region you were at the time."

The Middle East. He had been stationed at the NCIS Bahrain Field Office. A work weekend trip to Saudi had him at the US Embassy, and from the moment he had seen Eden, he had wanted her. He had pursued her, and for a month, they had spent all their off time together. That had ended when he'd found out she had been lying to him the entire time.

"I haven't had much interaction with Eden since that time."

"We know," Seth said. "It's just that if Green's death is linked to his work, you were there at the time. You might be able to give us some background."

"And with Eden Carlyle," Del said, pulling off the band-aid. The two team captains looked at him, and he shrugged. "Kap isn't dumb. He knew exactly what you were going after. We want you to go with Team Alpha to question Eden."

There was something in his voice that had Kap's senses tingling. "There's something you're not telling me."

Del looked at the captains again. "See, I told you. Not dumb." He turned back to look at Kap. "He had Eden's home address on a piece of paper. He also had her unlisted number. It's the one that Dillon Security gave her, and not a lot of people have access to that."

He absorbed that bit of information. "I'm not the person you want there. I irritate her."

And the moment he said it, he knew that he had told them more than he had wanted to. Rookie mistake.

"But you knew her once upon a time. You can tell us how she reacts to the news."

There was a long moment of silence as the pieces fell into place. "You want to know if she had anything to do with his murder. How was this Green killed?"

"Execution style, back of the head," Seth said.

"And y'all got the case because he was CIA?" he asked Adam. If he had worked for them for any amount of time, there could be dozens of people who might want him dead.

"Yes. HPD was thrilled to throw this at us," Adam said.

"Not sure how much I'll help, but I'll do what I can."

"Good. We're sending you with Graeme. He's the one she had the least amount of interaction with. We definitely don't want Autumn going, since her brother works as Eden's partner most of the time."

He nodded. "Just tell me when and I'll go."

There was a knock at the door, and he saw Graeme MacGregor standing there.

He fucking hated Mondays.

When they pulled up to the small house in Waimanalo, Kap ground his teeth. He was trying his best not to show just how much this was irritating him.

"You should stop grinding your teeth if you don't want your ex to know this irritates you."

He glanced over at the giant Scotsman. He was former military married to their ME, Elle.

"And maybe don't glare at your temporary partner."

"Sorry. This is still a sore subject with me."

"You don't say."

He heard the humor in Graeme's voice and couldn't help but smile.

"She's going to lie. It's what she does," Kap said, looking back at the house. Eden's family had a lot of money, so the modest house surprised him. He thought for sure she would live in one of the palatial beachfront mansions.

"CIA, I get it. Just don't say that to her face."

Kap slanted Graeme a look. "I won't."

The other man rolled his eyes. "Sure, you will. She's under your skin, and from my own personal experience, when feelings are involved, things can go awry. Just let me take the lead."

"No problem."

Graeme was muttering under his breath as he slipped out of the car.

Kap followed, his head pounding and his hands sweating. Why? Why did this woman still send his senses spiraling?

Graeme rang the doorbell, but there was no answer. After a few moments, he knocked on the door. Jesus, the man just did not know his own damned strength. The door vibrated with each hit of his fist.

"I'm coming, Jesus," someone grumbled. He knew that voice with a hint of Texas twang dripping from each syllable.

The door swung open, and he blinked.

Eden stood there, her hair a mess like she'd just woken up, and she was wearing a tank top and little sleep shorts.

"What the hell?" she grumbled, looking at Graeme. She hadn't noticed Kap yet. Hard to see him with a giant taking up most of the space.

He knew from personal experience that she liked to sleep in those little bitty shorts.

"We need to talk to you."

"We?"

Graeme moved so that she could see me. Her cheeks lost a little color when she saw Kap, but she didn't address him. Her gaze went back to Graeme.

"What do you want?"

"I thought people from Texas were supposed to be nice."

"Who the hell told you that? You know the state logo is *Don't Mess with Texas*, right? Especially when a Texan had about three hours of sleep. Wait? What time is it?"

"It's almost noon," Kap said.

"Okay, four hours and horrible jet lag."

Graeme sighed as if he was being put out. Kap rolled his eyes.

"Graeme would like to come in and talk to you about a case we're working. Your name came up."

She turned her attention to him, and he wanted to groan. Three years and all the lies she'd told him, and no other woman grabbed him by the balls with just a look. Her light blue eyes seemed to see more than he wanted to show her.

Then, she sighed and stepped back. They walked past her into the foyer, which led right into the living room. A large, grey sectional took up most of the room in front of a massive TV.

"What the fuck?" a male voice from up above bellowed.

"I don't have the bandwidth to deal with this," she muttered.

Kap looked up and saw a tall blond guy marching down the stairs. He was missing a shirt and was only wearing a pair of board shorts. In the last few months, he had run into Eden, but she had never had a man with her. Jealousy hit him harder than he would ever admit. Again, three years and she still got to him. So much so that Kap was thinking of punching the asshole for irritating Eden.

"What the hell are they doing here?"

"I don't know, and if you don't stop yelling, I will shoot you."

Kap blinked and looked at Eden. She sighed.

"El, this is Graeme MacGregor from TFH Team Alpha," she said, motioning to Graeme. Then she pointed at Kap. "The other one is Kap. Gentlemen, this is my brother Elwood."

El had reached the ground floor, and his eyes narrowed as he looked at Kap. He ignored Graeme. Great. El, the twin she'd talked about constantly. He was never a romantic rival, but Kap remembered being insanely irritated with their connection. It made sense since they were twins, but also the only children in the family.

"Did you just threaten to shoot your brother?" Graeme asked. Meanwhile, El was still staring at Kap, as if he were thinking about feeding him to sharks.

"Only fair. I have had no coffee, and I'm tired. Come on in the kitchen."

They followed her into the kitchen. She started an electric kettle, then grabbed a French press.

"What do you need?"

You.

Dammit. No. That was wrong.

He cleared his throat, which caused both Eden and Graeme to look at him.

"Your name is connected to our current case," he said.

She glanced at him, then at Graeme. "I got that already."

"What Kap is trying to say is that we were called to a murder scene of someone you know."

Her eyes narrowed. "Please. I'm tired. I landed at about three this morning from Japan. Just spit it out."

There was tension in her voice that had him on edge. Did she know what happened? Did she have anything to do with it?

"Andrew Green was found murdered," Graeme said.

Most people wouldn't notice the way her eyes flared and the little bit of color that leeched from her face. But he did. They may have been involved for only a month all those years ago, but he knew her better than any woman he had been involved with. That was why he was there. Graeme probably didn't even notice it.

"You worked with him," he said.

She shook her head. "Not directly. We knew each other because we were stationed in the same region. We had the same mentor."

"And that would be?" Graeme asked.

She stared at him as the kettle went off. After a few seconds, she finally grabbed the kettle and poured water into the French press.

"Ms. Carlyle, we need to know who that is."

She sighed, then looked at Kap. "You know I can't say."

That meant the mentor was still active.

"He was found here in Hawai'i?"

They both nodded.

"I didn't know he was here." She lifted her hands to rub her temple. "He didn't contact me."

"He had your cell phone number."

Her hands dropped, and she looked at them. "A lot of people have my number."

"This is your unlisted number with Dillon. I guess a lot of people don't have that one," Kap said.

He knew from what her partner had told them one time that all agents on assignments get a phone that is unlisted and almost impossible to trace and track.

She swallowed, another sign of her stress. "Do you know when Green came here?"

"No."

Team Alpha might know, but he had no idea, which helped with the questioning. He wasn't lying to her, and, normally, he wouldn't care about lying. But she was former CIA and a former lover. She would pick up on the lies.

"He never called me. I've been in Japan for the last week."

"Mix wasn't with you?" Graeme asked.

Mix was her usual partner. His real name was Ian Smith, the brother of Autumn Bradford, a Team Alpha member. This was going to be so damned messy.

"No. He picked up a job with *Task Force Honolulu*. I had already been approved for a job in Japan. Emily is working with him."

"Who were you protecting in Japan?"

She blinked, then shook her head. "Talk to Dillon. If they say I can brief you, then I will. Otherwise, I signed an NDA. I can't say anything without their approval."

"This is a murder investigation," Graeme said, irritation threading his Scottish brogue.

"I understand, and I will happily tell you where I was if you call Dillon to get approval. I need coffee first and a shower because I feel like I have traveling crud on me still."

He knew she wasn't lying, or he thought she wasn't. But there was something she wasn't telling them.

"Can you take a guess at why he had your number?" Kap asked.

She shook her head. "I'm not sure, unless he was trying to get a job with Dillon."

Which would make sense. Dillon Security was one of the

world's top security agencies. There was still something there, something that she wasn't telling them. And that pissed him off. This was a murder investigation, and she was fucking around.

"He had your *unlisted* number," Kap said, unable to keep the anger from bubbling up.

She shrugged, but he noticed the tension in her shoulders. "I don't know. He *was* CIA."

"Former," Kap said.

Her eyes widened. "He left the CIA?"

That was a genuine reaction, although Kap wasn't sure. She had lived a lie most of her life, so it was second nature to her.

"You didn't keep up with him?" Graeme asked.

She shook her head. "We had the same mentor, but we didn't work much together. I was kept away from many known operatives because I was considered more of an asset. Andrew was...well, he was sloppy at best." She sighed. "I did suspect him of being one of the people who might have outed me."

"We'll need proof you were off the island."

She nodded. "You can talk to Dillon. I flew back with the client, so they will have to get his approval."

"Your brother? Was he here?" Kap asked.

"No. He was on the job with me. Why he's here with me still, I have no idea."

Graeme chuckled. "Not fun living together?"

"We might be twins, but he's still my little brother."

"By five minutes, Eden," her brother said as he walked into the kitchen. He was dressed now, or at least he'd put on a shirt.

"We'll be talking to Dillon," Graeme said.

She nodded. "I'll be waiting to hear from them. I'll happily come into TFH when they give me permission." Which meant that whoever she traveled with had Dillon sign an NDA, which wasn't that unusual. Celebrities and the wealthy often preferred to keep many aspects of their lives out of the public eye.

"What happened?" El asked.

She glanced at them, and Kap nodded, letting her know she could tell her brother. One thing about Eden was that she knew how an investigation had to proceed.

"Andrew Green was found murdered."

His eyebrows rose in surprise. That's when Kap realized he and Eden shared the same light blue eyes.

"Green?" He looked at Graeme and Kap. "He was on the island? That's weird."

"Why?"

"He was all about the Middle East. He could even speak Arabic and Farsi."

"You knew him?"

"Briefly. He was a bit annoying. Like he was always trying to impress people with his language skills and the fact that his uncle had been in the CIA." He shrugged. "That's a dangerous habit when you're working undercover."

He was right. That must be what Eden meant about him being sloppy. Eden would never accept that since she had been so damned good at hiding her real job from him.

"He left the CIA," Eden said. "Had you heard that?"

El shook his head. "Wow. I thought he would never leave. He would brag about his uncle, saying he would move up the chain fast. I think he saw himself as a section chief, which we all knew wouldn't happen."

"We?" Kap asked.

"Everyone who talked to him. Bragging is the kiss of death as a spy. But both Eden and I are considered out of the circle of trust."

"We'll probably want both of you to come in," Graeme said.

They both nodded. "Get us the all clear from Dillon, and I will happily come in."

She gave them her number and saw them to the door.

"If you think of anything, let us know," Graeme said.

She gave Graeme a blinding smile that had Kap curling his fingers into his palms. Even knowing she was doing it to divert Graeme's attention, it irritated Kap. Again, the acid taste of jealousy hit him hard. Graeme had no interest in her, though. First, she was tied to their case, and second, he was insanely in love with his wife, their ME.

"I sure will," she said, injecting more of her Texas accent into her voice. Yep, she was trying to divert them.

Graeme headed for the SUV, but Kap lingered. It had nothing to do with the fact that he still dreamed about her. No, he knew without a doubt, she was lying to them. Maybe not outright, but she wasn't being completely honest.

"We'll find out what you're hiding, Eden."

She studied him. "A woman has the right to a few secrets."

"You call them secrets. I call them lies."

Her smile dissolved. "Yeah, you keep telling yourself that, Kappy."

Fuck, he hated when she used that name. "You see it differently, I'm sure."

"Interesting. I have a question for you. Have you worked deep undercover?"

"That's not the same."

"Answer the question. Unless you're afraid to."

"Yes."

"And even if you met someone you liked while you were undercover, would you blow that cover?"

"It wasn't the same."

"No, it wasn't. I have a feeling that you had no idea what was on the line."

"I have a good idea."

"Oh, do you? When you were undercover, was your entire family at risk? Did one of your sisters get into service and help you with your undercover work?" He said nothing. "No. They didn't. So forgive me for not telling you everything the moment we met."

Kap knew she was right, that she definitely had done her job just like any other undercover operative had.

"We were together for four weeks and you never said—"

"This argument is old. You're pissed that I wasn't completely truthful with you from the moment we met. Do you remember what I told you?"

You don't want to get involved with me, Hanson.

"Yeah, you do," she said, as she studied his expression. She shook her head, suddenly looking as if she was exhausted. "I'm sure Dillon will call me when they clear me to talk to you."

Without another word, she stepped back and slammed the door in his face.

He pulled in a deep breath and released it before heading

to the SUV. When he stepped up into the vehicle, Graeme gave him a second before he started asking questions.

"So, do you think she knows something?"

He studied the front of the house.

"Oh, she knows something, but not sure what it is or how it fits into the broader story."

Because the one thing he knew about Eden was that there was always more to the story.

two

EDEN SHUT the door and leaned back against it. Her entire body was flushed with a mix of excitement and fear. It was an unusual combination that left her feeling dizzy. How did he seem to get better-looking every time she saw him? Kapone Hanson was a tall drink of water, and she always felt thirsty around him.

After three years, she should be over him. He'd walked away from her fast enough. When her world was falling apart, she had gone to him. It had been the worst decision of her life. Even in that moment when he was accusing her of being a whore for the CIA, she had wanted him. She wanted nothing more than to see him smile, feel his body against hers...and he had looked at her like she was a traitor.

He had captured her attention from the beginning. He'd stepped into the ballroom in the embassy, and her entire body had sizzled. Standing over six feet tall, he had green eyes, short dark hair, and dark brown skin. He was built, but more along a streamlined kind of body like a swimmer, and she had fallen for him from the start. Stupidest move of her life.

She stepped into the kitchen and frowned at her French press. It looked like sludge.

"That looks gross, Ed."

She rolled her eyes at her brother. "Tell me something I don't know."

"That Kap knows you were lying."

"I know," she said, her nerves still pinging. It was the same reaction she'd had to him every time they'd interacted. It was the pain. The pain that he'd caused by his own betrayal. And like an idiot, she still wanted him. Needing something to do with her hands, she started cleaning her press out and turned on the kettle again.

"But you said you would go in and talk to them."

"I said we both would, so maybe not be an asshole to the people who are investigating the death of one of our suspects."

"You told them you suspected him."

A statement, not a question. El was really good at eavesdropping. It had been one of his greatest talents when they were kids. Once they started working for *The Company*, he used it to his advantage. Now, he worked a lot of corporate espionage cases, and she was sure he used it to his advantage there as well.

"They would have made the connection. It's Task Force Hawai'i. It's better to let them know that I personally suspected him."

He sat on one of the chairs at the breakfast bar. "So I guess we mark him off the list."

She nodded as she thought about all of their suspects. "I wonder if Marv knows."

Her brother made a rude noise. Marvin Bellows had

been her mentor. He was a family friend, known as Uncle Marv to both of them. Since the incident in Saudi, her brother had been suspicious of everyone who wasn't family. *Real family.* Meaning their parents and them. That was it, and she didn't blame him. After decades of service to the country, their family had been sold out to the highest bidder. Their lives had been in danger from that moment on.

After pressing the coffee, she poured each of them a cup.

"Come on."

She didn't have to tell him where they were headed. One of the reasons she had bought this house was the hidden room beneath the stairs. She knew it would be perfect to hide her investigation.

El followed her, a silent dark cloud surrounding him. He blamed himself, but it wasn't his fault. If anyone was to blame, it was Eden. She was the one who'd slipped up, somehow. Whoever this was had outed her. Yes, they had gone after her brother, but that was to draw her out. She was positive she had been a target.

She opened the hidden panel of buttons and pressed the code to open the door. It creaked open, and she slid it open the rest of the way. The lights came on automatically as they stepped in. El walked over to the board and crossed out Green's name.

"You never thought it was him," she said.

"No. He was a mess, but I never got the vibe that he would go after people he worked with."

She stepped up next to him, then took a long, healthy sip of her coffee. In the past, there had always been people who wanted to sell out *The Company*. There was more than the public knew about because, well, the CIA is filled with a bunch of secretive bastards. It was the nature of the beast.

"Had you heard Green was in Hawai'i?" she asked.

"No. I guess it was a good idea to move here after all."

"They said he had my number with Dillon."

She felt his gaze roam over her. Eden and El had always had that twin thing, until El's weekend in hell. Both of them were still dealing with his PTSD.

"Not hard for an ex-CIA agent," he murmured.

She knew he was correct. They both had a multitude of contacts who could help them, including one she hoped her partner at Dillon never found out about. He would not be happy about it.

"I guess I need to call Dillon and let them know."

He nodded. "That will probably be lover boy's next stop."

She let that comment go by. El had feelings about Kap. Sooo many feelings, even though this was the first time they had ever met. Men. Always screwing up her plans.

This was supposed to be a lovely week, one where she could go to the beach and act like a normal person. Or even fly back to see her folks in Texas. She glanced at her twin as he wrote the word Hawai'i with a question mark behind it. This was the second former operative who had been murdered in Hawai'i. Knowing TFH, it wouldn't take them long to figure it out.

"I'll call it in, then get cleaned up and go on in."

"You know Conner won't make you do that," El said.

"No, but there needs to be a thorough investigation, and it starts with my phone."

"Should we tell Conner?" El asked.

She shook her head. "The problem is ex operatives get whacked all the time. We both know that."

Both of them knew people who had run into old enemies after retirement. One of them usually ended up dead.

Once she was in her bedroom, she grabbed her burner phone.

> Eden: Take Green off your list.

> Sam: Why? Did El kill him?

> Eden: No.

> Sam: Did you kill him?

> Eden: Why would you ask me that in a text?

> Sam: That's not a no.

Then her phone rang.

"Listen, I have to take a shower and get to work."

"I thought you were off for a week."

"Yeah, that's all fucked up. Green was murdered last night, or, well, the body was found last night. Not sure when he was killed."

"And you have to go in for what reason?"

"He had my Dillon phone number."

"Ah, well, if he had one of mine—which we know no one is as good as me, but there are a few that get close—he would be able to find that out easily."

"TFH was here. They sent Kap."

Silence. Silence from Sam was always dangerous. She had

a genius-level IQ, and she definitely plotted things Eden never wanted to think about. That's why she asked Eden if either she or her brother had killed Green.

"It isn't his team's job. They only investigate under a few circumstances. So, TFH is playing head games, sending him over with the big Scottish dude."

"I agree, so make sure you're only talking and texting on this number. They're probably going to confiscate your other phones," Sam said.

Yes, she had a lot of phones, but once you've been a CIA agent and you were raised by them, it was second nature to be that secretive."

"El thinks we need to look at Hawai'i and why two operatives were here," Eden said.

"And why they were on the list?"

She sighed. "See if you can find out Green's movements before he ended up here. He should be easy to track. That dude sucked at being an agent."

Sam would know. She was never an agent, just an analyst with an intelligence pedigree that even Eden found overwhelming. When you have family in both the CIA and MI-6, you are considered somewhat untouchable. Well, until you weren't.

Which is why Sam had been in hiding for over two years. When El had disappeared, Sam was the person Eden had gone to. Eden had known that Sam could find anyone. What she hadn't expected was that Sam would be targeted.

"He did. I didn't know he had left *The Company*."

The clicking of keys reached her over the phone, and she knew that Sam was searching. Yes, she could still hack into the CIA, which is why she probably scared the fuck out of them.

"Yeah. He retired two months ago. Or, well, quit. The rumor was that he had a job with a big security company."

She wasn't about to ask her friend how she'd found that out. The truth was that she had probably hacked into texts between coworkers.

"That's the theory I gave them. I thought maybe he was looking for a job."

"So, you didn't tell them that you're hunting for a possible serial killer?"

"No. That would make both El and me suspects for all of the murders."

"You probably have alibis for at least some of them."

"What are the chances that El and I would have alibis for each one, or it would look like we're hunting people and killing them?"

"Okay, you're probably right." There was a long beat of silence, and Eden knew what was coming. "So, how is Mix doing? Is he still being a prig?"

She chuckled. Yes, she shouldn't be amused by it, but the rivalry between her partner Ian Smith (aka Mix) and Sam was funny. It went back to both their days working for intelligence agencies. Sam never let him forget that she had the upper hand.

"He is not a prig with anyone but you."

Sam snorted. "Are you going to work with him on that show?"

Ian was working on *Task Force Honolulu*. Apparently, they were having issues with security, and the star of the show, Jakob Wulf, was a billionaire who could afford protection until the network got their asses in gear.

"Probably not until next week, if he's still working with them."

There was clicking on the keys again.

"You're texting him right now, aren't you?"

"Of course. He needs to be taken down a peg."

It wasn't that Sam didn't think he was a good agent. When Eden had started working at Dillon, Sam researched the former MI-6 agent. Sam had said he was a good guy, even though Eden thought she might not be telling her everything. There seemed to be something about when he left MI-6, but as usual, Sam was keeping it close to her chest. The woman had a vault of secrets. Eden was probably her best friend, but there was still so much she didn't know about her friend.

She did know her real name.

"Delilah Eddington Underwood."

"Do not three name me with my real name. Especially with that Texas twang and using that horrible full first name. I don't need anyone to hear my real name."

Eden rolled her eyes.

"El is the only person here, and you know you can trust him. "

She made a noise. "I'm not worried about that. I'm worried that you might be under surveillance."

"TFH hasn't had time for a search warrant."

Sam sighed. "No. I don't like the fact that things seemed to be converging on Hawai'i."

That gave Eden pause. "You think it has to do with El and me?"

"Yes. Or at least that's a possibility. How do we know that O'Malley and Green didn't have something to do with these murders?"

Eden was sure El was thinking the same thing. Edwin O'Malley, another former agent, had been murdered three months earlier. They were pretty sure he had been operating as a double agent until he left the CIA. Then he turned up dead in Hawai'i.

They were running out of suspects.

"We don't know. Hell, maybe we have it all wrong."

"We don't. The pattern is there."

She sighed. She knew her friend was right. "It would be much better if it were just a bunch of unconnected murders."

"No. Then we wouldn't be able to figure out who took El, then outed you. Also, wouldn't you rather have one person involved in the murders and all that shit, than it being a bunch of people running around offing ex-CIA agents?"

"Okay, you have a point."

"Of course I do."

Eden snorted. "Please, don't overwhelm me with your modesty."

"My grandmother told me it was a waste of time to be modest when I was made to stand out."

"I'll let you know what Dillon Security finds out."

"Gotcha. Stay safe."

"Ditto."

After she hung up, she pushed through the jet lag and irritation of TFH trying to play head games with her and hurried to get ready. The faster she got to Dillon, the faster she would find out what the hell was going on.

Ninety minutes after she called in the breach, Eden was striding into Dillon Security. Dillon was actually headquartered in Miami, Florida, but Conner had moved to Hawai'i a few years ago. It made sense to open an office here, as they had a significant amount of international business.

"Hey, lady," Emily Daniels said as she walked down the hallway.

The Dillon operative usually worked from the office, being the techie that she was. Every now and then, she went out to work in corporations like El did—sometimes with him. She was tall and athletic, with dark hair braided over her shoulder. She shared the same unusual shade of eyes as her brother, former MMA fighter Aaron Daniels.

"Hey, yourself."

"I thought you were off this week."

"So you haven't heard?"

"What? Is Devon Stryker dead? Did you fuck up the protection job?"

Emily's voice was filled with humor because Eden was sure the other woman knew they had arrived home safely.

"No. I had to come in because of some issue with my phone."

"That's why the boss showed up a few minutes ago. He was cranky."

"Is TFH here yet?"

She shook her head and stepped up beside Eden as she started down the hallway to Conner's office. He was the owner, but he only worked a few days a week, preferring to do most of his work from home. His wife was a published author, and he occasionally took care of the kids so she could focus on her work. Nothing is as sexy as a strong Alpha male type helping his partner.

She pushed that idea aside. In the last three years, she had come to understand that she would never have that. With the constant target on her back, she couldn't ask a man to put his life on the line for that, too.

"Oh, you are having bad thoughts. What did Elwood do now?"

She glanced at her friend. "Nothing. Well, other than being El."

"So, doom and gloom and pissy. Got it."

Emily whipped out her phone and started texting him. Her brother and Emily had a complicated relationship. Eden knew that her brother was half in love with the woman, but since those horrible forty-eight hours, he felt he had nothing to offer a woman.

"Did you just yell at him in a text?"

"No. I just told him he was a whiny ass titty baby."

A bubble of laughter tickled the back of her throat. No one could put her brother in his place like Emily. He *was* morose. Granted, they all knew what had made him that way. Well, not the particulars, but they knew he had been captured by terrorists. No one but Eden knew how broken her brother was when she'd found him. Even his worst days, when he danced on the borderline between insanity and sanity, were better than she had ever expected after those few dark weeks after he had been rescued.

They walked into Conner's outer office. There were two actual offices there. One was Conner's. The other belonged to Lucius "Luc" Warner, the man who ran the office. The ex-SEAL was a good boss, if a little grumpy.

"Hey, ladies," Junie Monroe said. She was their executive assistant, and all of them knew she was the one running the company. She had been with them for only two months, and Eden didn't know if they could keep running if Junie left.

In her early thirties, the woman seemed to walk in and take over everything. It was weird seeing the way she ordered people around, considering the woman was barely five feet three inches tall.

"They're waiting for you, Eden." Then she looked at Emily. "Not you."

"You're no fun."

She rolled her eyes. "Go on, Eden. Emily, they need you to help with some issues they're having with security on the set."

"Oh, goodie. Do I get to go?"

Junie nodded. "So go mess with Mix, but please, don't be rude to the actors. They have a lot of pull with the studio, and Conner wants to make sure that we have a good working relationship."

"Hey, as long as I can mess with Mix, I'm good. See ya."

Then she abandoned Eden.

"Go on," Junie said, motioning with her hand.

Squaring her shoulders, Eden walked over to the door, gave it a knock, then opened it.

"Come in, Eden," Conner said.

Their boss—the owner of the whole damned company—was in his mid-forties and still in fantastic shape. He was former FBI who broke out and started his own company and became a wealthy man in the process. He had definite zaddie vibes, with a bit of grey at his temples and laugh lines around his mouth and eyes.

Warner was...not as happy with life. Granted, he was an

excellent boss. He liked order in the office, and he never questioned whether a woman could do the same job as a man. Almost six five, he probably wasn't as big as when he'd served. There were rumors that he had been a member of SEAL Team Six, but, of course, no one knew for sure.

He had blond hair—still in a buzz cut—dark eyes, and preferred to wear polo shirts and jeans to work.

"Sorry you had to come in on your week off," Conner said. Warner said nothing. "We could have done this over the phone."

"No. We need to have someone look at the phone. I want to know how someone found out my number," she said.

"All of us want that. Have a seat. Let's talk about this Green."

She did as he requested and fought the need to rub her hands down her pant legs because they were so damned wet.

"What do you want to know about him?"

"What kind of agent was he?" Warner asked.

"He sucked. No. Wait. He was decent enough, but he was sloppy." She shrugged one shoulder. "You know that can be the difference between life and death when you work for *The Company*. He liked to brag."

Conner nodded. "He couldn't do something like find an unlisted number."

She shook her head. "He was...well, he did a little undercover work, but mostly he worked for my mentor."

She didn't say Marv's name because Conner knew who she was talking about.

"Do you know why he was here?"

She shook her head, and it was the truth. Had he been there to kill her, help her, or ask her to help him get a job?

"I talked to someone I used to work with, and she said the rumor was he had a job lined up. Or maybe planned to have one. Not sure, but apparently, he thought that there was more money in the private sector."

"And he would be correct." When he said nothing else, she fought the urge to fill in the silence. Having been raised by two spies, she knew better than to jump in. "Are you and El working another angle?"

"No. We have no dog in the hunt, as my grandfather would say. The two of us were outed, so the truth is we just try to avoid people who might want us dead."

That was true enough that she didn't even flinch when she said it.

His phone buzzed on the desk. He looked down. "TFH is already here."

Her heart jumped into her throat.

"What?"

She drew in a deep breath. "TFH is using my ex in the investigation. It irritates me."

"Yeah, and it's smart. Tell you what. Go through the other door into Warner's office."

"I don't run away."

His mouth kicked up on one side. "I know, but I also know you aren't telling me everything."

She opened her mouth, but he held his hand up. "I don't want to know unless it involves this job."

She shook her head.

"I don't want them talking to you. You weren't here when the guy was murdered."

"You have a TOD?"

He glanced at Warner. "I...took a peek at their investigation. The guy was killed sometime before midnight. Both you and your brother were just landing."

She sighed as relief trickled through her system. "And El stayed at my place last night."

"Good. Now go."

As she stepped into Warner's office, she let the door shut behind her and waited. The truth was, she didn't like scurrying away, but she understood the need for a strategic retreat. She needed to regroup and figure out what the hell was going on.

three

BY THE TIME Kap and Graeme returned from the Dillon Security offices, he wanted to break something. He knew he should be holding onto his temper, but this case was already testing every one of his nerves.

"So?" Adam asked as they stepped into the common room.

"They wouldn't tell us where she or her brother had been and told us to get a search warrant for the phone," Graeme said.

"You don't sound worried," Kap said.

He shrugged. "Dillon's former FBI. He's just going by the book. We should receive the warrant soon. Right?"

Adam nodded. "And remember, if someone paid enough for her and her brother to protect them outside of the country, that's some big money. Dillon is one of the most expensive security companies. Whoever it was will have to be notified. You know there is an NDA."

"Which Dillon said they were doing, but apparently, the client hadn't responded. Of course, they got back in the dead of night," Graeme said, studying him. "They showed us the proof."

Yep, they had been ready with that, which wasn't suspicious at all. All agents had their own security systems, so they could pull up the proof of the brother and sister returning.

"Is it normal for her brother to stay over with her?" Adam asked.

"Apparently, when they fly in like that. He has a place on one of the other islands, so he usually stays at her place when he has work here," Graeme said. "If she didn't have proof that he went into the house with her, I would put my money more on him than on her."

Kap's gaze narrowed as he studied Graeme. "Why?"

He shrugged. "He has that look about him. He's living on the edge. There's a lot of darkness there."

He knew what the Scotsman was saying. Former special forces for the British military, Graeme had witnessed many terrible things and the harm they could inflict on many people.

"While we are waiting on the warrant, and whoever their client was, start running down people who might know something about why that man was on our island. People like him just don't pop up in places for no reason."

They both nodded and headed to their offices. Unfortunately, Kap's teammates followed him in.

"So, this has to do with Eden?" Rami said.

Dammit. He needed a break. Dealing with his anger each time he encountered Eden was becoming annoying. More annoying? His teammates fucking with him.

"Yes."

"How did she look?"

"Like always."

But she hadn't looked the same as usual. There was a fragility about her now. It was like the morning she'd returned to Saudi when he had confronted her, like one wrong word and she would fall apart.

Nikki studied him. "I heard her brother was there."

Of course, she had. TFH was a rumor mill, complete with bets being made on everything from who was going to hook up with whom to who was going to get married.

"Wait, are there bets on me?"

"Yep," Nikki said, popping the "p."

"The fuck?"

"Everyone is wondering how long you'll last before Graeme kicks you to the curb," Rami said with a chuckle.

"So, there isn't a bet about them banging?"

Dammit, he knew that voice. Their captain's fiancée was a little different. Autumn Bradford leaned against the doorjamb. She was eating, of course. Some kind of candy bar. He had no idea how she stayed so thin when she ate enough food for a small family of three. Probably had something to do with being raised in a cult. He'd heard Seth comment that she would go weeks without a decent meal, so now she ate whatever and whenever she wanted.

"Not that I know about," Nikki said.

"Uh, weird. So, she has an alibi, but that dude was CIA, so you know what that means."

The feds were going to show up, if they hadn't already been in contact with TFH. That meant more headaches.

He knew he should have realized that was coming, but within a few seconds, his phone went off.

Captain: Big Boss's office, now.

"Well, this has been fun, but I have a meeting."

"No one has ever said that. No one has ever said they *want* to go to a meeting," Autumn said.

He said nothing to that. Instead, he shooed them out of his office, then hurried to Del's office.

Adam, Graeme, and Seth were already there. Del did not look happy.

"Shut the door, Kap," he said.

He did, then turned to face the other three men.

"What happened?"

"We have an issue."

"The CIA?"

Del nodded. "Here's the thing. They're acting really weird."

"They're the CIA. They *are* weird," Graeme murmured.

"This is over the top. They asked questions, and I told them I would share if they would. They refused."

"That's not that odd for them," Seth said.

"You think there is more to this than just a normal killing?" Adam asked.

Del nodded.

"There's never a simple killing when it comes to an operative," Kap said. "Are they taking over?"

"No. That's the bizarre part. You've dealt more with them when you were with NCIS than I have, so can you ever remember a time when they didn't try to take over?"

"They always want to take over, even when it's clear that the death of an agent—either active or retired—has nothing to do with their work at the CIA. They use the excuse of national security."

Del leaned back in his chair and studied them all. "I don't like this shit. It feels like there's something nasty festering, and the fucking CIA dragged it to Hawai'i."

"You two couldn't get anything from Eden or her brother?" Adam asked.

"No," Graeme said. "In fact, Kap and his pretty mug seemed to irritate her."

Yes, let's talk about my ex and how much I irritate her.

"Do you think Kap should stand down?" Adam asked.

"No. He knocks her off kilter. We know she probably was telling the truth about when she returned to the island, but I think she knows more. Kap agrees with me on that."

"Dig into this Green. I want to know everywhere he was stationed."

"The CIA is helping us with that one?" Kap asked, not able to keep the skepticism out of his voice.

"No. But I know that Charity has been digging into his background. We might also want to try to call in that friend of Jin's," he said to Adam. Jin was Adam's fiancée. "See if she can get hold of Sam."

He nodded. "Graeme, you and Kap head down to see what you can find out."

Ordered away from the office, Eden made her way to the set of *Task Force Honolulu*. Emily had made it to the set, just to be called back to help work on how Green had found out Eden's number.

She stepped on set, flashed her ID, and found Ian right away.

The man could be a model. He fit in this world, with its lights and cameras, thanks to his classic good looks, dark hair, and blue eyes; he could definitely play the role that Jakob Wulf played.

She caught his eye as she made her way over to him and the actor in question. Wulf was one of the three Wulf siblings who owned and operated Wulf Industries. Although he seemed to spend more time acting than with the company.

"Eden Carlyle," he said, rising from his director's chair. He leaned forward, giving her a kiss on her cheek. "It's good to see you again."

"Thanks," she said. She and Ian had worked protection for Jakob's fiancée last year when she'd had a stalker. "It's good to see you, too. How's Lani?"

"Brilliant."

He didn't hide his accent when he was off camera. He was playing a good old American, but he was as British as her partner.

There was a call, and Jakob sighed. "Back to work. Make sure to get some of the snacks, Eden."

Then he headed back to what looked like a scene they were filming in front of one of the hotels.

Ian stepped closer. "You look like shite."

"Fuck off," she said with no heat. He was another brother she didn't need, but she appreciated his concern. "I got no sleep, then had the damned TFH at my door this morning."

"Yeah. I heard from my nemesis."

"Oh, you talked to Sam?"

She hadn't told him that the woman he knew as Sam was probably her best friend outside of her brother. She didn't like divulging secrets to anyone, even people she trusted. Either way, everyone knew he had a rivalry going on with the former CIA analyst. Not just at Dillon. Apparently, most of TFH was aware of it as well.

"No. I meant Emily."

"You have more than one?"

He pursed his lips but said nothing for a moment. She knew he was trying to get hold of his temper.

"Anything going on here?"

"Naw. They should have sufficient security in place by the end of the week. Jakob wants us to do the background checks since the last one showed up naked in his dressing room."

"Jesus. I hadn't heard that."

He chuckled. "The best part was that Lani was the one who found her. I don't think that woman will be doing anything like that ever again."

Lani Kingston-Wulf was Hawaiian born and tough. She could just imagine how the woman reacted.

They watched the scene being filmed, which she barely paid attention to. Instead, she kept an eye on the people surrounding the actors as they worked through their scene. And, of course, she was thinking about Green's murder. The man wasn't anyone who was in the know about things going on. Yes, he was an agent, but she knew the only reason he had the job was that he was a legacy. His uncle had been a section chief.

Ian tapped her arm and motioned with his head to a small area away from the filming. She followed him.

"What's up?"

"What do you mean?"

"You're thinking about something else."

"I can do my job, Ian."

"I wasn't saying you couldn't. I just know something else is going on. I know you had to multitask in your former career because you actually had two jobs."

Now that she was outed, everyone knew that her job with her family's business was a cover. It didn't mean that she didn't have work to do, tedious office work that often made her want to scream. Eden still had to do it.

"Well, it has nothing to do with this job, so don't worry about it."

He studied her for a moment. He was one of those kinds of guys who had women turning their heads as they walked past him. The movie star looks caught their attention, but this look now would scare the hell out of any woman who thought he would be a fun guy.

"Stop looking at me like I'm a suspect."

His mouth twitched. They worked together well because they understood that digging around in their pasts wasn't something their partner should do.

Maybe that was changing. If so, she would need a new partner, and she hated that. She and Ian had the same work ethic.

"It has to do with this guy having your phone number. Did you know him well?"

She shrugged. "Not that well. I mean, we knew each other because we worked in the same region, but not that well."

"So not a former lover?"

She snorted, then sobered. "No. I was involved with one

man the four years I worked in the Middle East for obvious reasons."

Ian nodded, understanding filling his eyes. It was easier when you were undercover and not the public face of your family's business. Or at least, she thought it might be. She had never lived that way. Ever.

"I know that it isn't easy to deal with being in the limelight either at large or just in the organization."

Ian had also grown up the way she had. Her father was a legend in MI-6. Both of them had dealt with expectations from their parents and the organization as a whole. It was a lot to deal with, but at least she had El. Until his father had found out that Autumn was actually his daughter, Ian had grown up with no siblings.

She nodded. "Anyway, I didn't know him that well. He had the same monitoring agent, of course."

"Does he have anything to do with that O'Malley who was murdered?"

For a second, she felt her breath freeze in her lungs. "Hmm? O'Malley?"

"Stop the act, Eden. I knew Edwin. Nasty bit of goods."

She rolled her shoulders. "I'm not sure. I just don't know what's happening. It's almost like someone is killing people to cover something up, if you know what I mean."

And she knew from his expression, he did. "Yeah, I was thinking the same thing. When Emily told me his name, I remembered he was an agent in your region. Do you think it has anything to do with your outing?"

"Truthfully, I'm not so sure. Why wait this long? That doesn't make any sense."

"People rarely make sense, especially spies."

"What makes you think it's a spy?"

He gave her a look of disgust. "Don't treat me like I'm stupid."

"Sorry."

And she was. She liked Ian. He was one of the partners she'd had who she felt understood her.

"Trust me. I can help you."

She did trust him, but there was something else that bothered her. "You could be put at risk."

He rolled his eyes. "I can bloody well handle anything they have."

"Really? Because that's what El thought too."

He pursed his lips as he studied her for a long, uncomfortable moment. Usually, long moments of silence didn't bother her, but she felt the weight of her partner's irritation. Then, his face cleared.

"You care about me, and you're trying to protect me. I'll have to tell Autumn because she still isn't sure about you."

Autumn Bradford was a thorn in her side. She had boldly questioned Eden about whether Ian could trust her. Granted, she would do the same to anyone who worked with her brother, but he was more of a lone wolf than a partner type. At least, these days he was. The only person he would work with other than Eden was Emily, and Eden knew she could trust her.

"Anyway, there is no reason for that. We'll have drinks after work."

Then he strode away as if his announcement changed everything. She hurried after him.

"I don't do drinks."

"That's okay. You can drive."

She could fight it, but Ian could be tenacious. She would just have to come up with something before then. Sam said she could trust Ian, and she had never steered Eden wrong. But everyone who would help her would be drawn into the danger, and Eden would feel responsible if Ian got hurt.

El sat in his car down the street from TFH headquarters. He wasn't happy with the situation, and he was more than a little pissed that Hanson was back in Eden's life because of this mess. When El found out that he was on the island, he had moved to the area. Eden was strong, but that man had always been her weakness. If he had stood by her all those years ago, El would be happy for her to be with him. Instead, Hanson had turned his back on her, broken her when she had been at her lowest.

That was something El would never forgive, and it put Hanson in the "don't trust" category. So, he sat in his car, his gaze trained on the front door, waiting for him and his 'partner' to come out.

He was so intent on watching the door that when someone knocked on the passenger door window, he jumped. Fuck. Rookie mistake.

Emily bent down to eye level with him. He didn't immediately unlock the door, so her eyebrow raised. Dammit, he didn't need her here. Not that she wasn't a good agent. She was smarter than many people gave her credit for, which worked to her advantage in the field. That high IQ was a problem when he was around her because she tended to mess with his concentration. Nothing that she did in particular. Just existing in his orbit seemed to leave him befuddled.

With reluctance, he unlocked the door.

"That was very rude," she said in way of greeting as she settled in the passenger seat.

"How did you find me?"

"You have a Dillon Security car. I just looked ya up."

"I dismantled..."

She laughed. "Like there's only one of them on the cars. I would never let that happen."

His hands tightened on the steering wheel. He loved her laugh. It was filled with joy...something he had not experienced a lot of in the last three years.

"Did the boss send you?"

"Naw. He's spending time with his lawyers discussing the search warrant that we all know is coming. Just so you know, Devon Stryker said he'd swear that you were with them."

"We were."

"I know. Just keeping you updated since you turned off your phone. Your sister got my gig, and since I was done for the day, I thought I should find you and make sure you aren't fucking up your life."

He blinked. "What do you mean?"

She rolled her eyes. "I have three older brothers, so I understand your species. I know that you are sitting down the street from TFH, where your sister's ex works."

He said nothing.

"Listen, I get it. I would do the same thing. There was this girl one time who was really trying to fuck with Aaron. You know he's a big teddy bear."

El did not know that. Aaron Daniels won the MMA

World Title three years in a row before he retired. The man was a machine in the ring, and thinking of him as a teddy bear was just insane.

"See, she thought she could use him for money. Think about it. He had all those endorsements and, well, she thought she could bleed him dry. I knew there was something up about her from the start. Not that I would think any woman wouldn't be lucky to get any of my brothers, just that there was something off about her. So, I researched her."

"You used your Dillon access?"

"Naw, I was in college. That skank was wanted in Utah for owing her ex thousands of dollars."

"What did Aaron say? Did he get mad at you?"

"Tsk, tsk. I didn't tell him. That would have just upset him. I called the authorities and had her arrested. See, that ex? He had been her boss, and the thousands had been embezzled."

He blinked. "He had no idea you turned her in?"

"Nope. I saved my brother and kept his pride intact."

This was the exact reason he worried about her. She was so damned clever.

"Like I said, I get it. Your sister is still infatuated with him. And he's hung up on her."

El snorted. "He abandoned her."

She tilted her head. Damn, she was pretty. He loved smart women, and she fit the bill. Tall, with long, dark hair and blue eyes, she always seemed to be able to see more than most people.

"I get that. We all make mistakes, El. One decision can alter your life and the lives of people you care about. One day, everything is fine, and one little decision can leave your world in smithereens."

There was a note in her voice that left his blood cold. He studied her profile, trying to discern what she was actually saying.

"Don't. You won't like what you find," she said. Then she looked at him, gave him that blinding smile of hers. "So, how long are we staying here today?"

He sighed. "Until they leave for the day."

"And what is our objective?"

He blinked at her.

"Because if it's intimidation, that's a bad idea, cowboy. You could be charged with obstruction of justice. Then your sister would be on her own. That would be bad."

His eyes narrowed. "What do you mean?"

"Absolutely nothing. Seriously. But it's a vibe I have. Bad juju dancing around you and Eden. She needs you by her side. Don't fuck that up."

Fuck, she was right. What the hell was he trying to prove by being here?

"I get it, like I said, but we can only go so far protecting the people we love. Sometimes, the live and learn aspect is the most important part of a relationship that fails."

"You just said you turned in your brother's girlfriend."

"First of all, she was wanted for a felony. Second of all, I'm cool with Aaron dealing with his own girlfriends. If you saw how many women he had while he was fighting..." she rolled her eyes. "And even now. Not that I'm a prude, it's just gross thinking about my brother that way."

"But you turned her in."

"Because of the financial aspect of it. Treat my brother

like the skank he is? I'm okay with that. But go after his money? Fuck that."

Before he could respond, his phone rang. It was a blocked number. Only one other person had his burner cell number.

"What the fuck are you doing outside of TFH?" Lila, aka Sam, demanded.

"Funny thing, Emily asked the same question."

"That's because she's brilliant. I know you want to make Hanson pay for hurting your sister, but we both know what's going on."

Yeah. Guilt. If he hadn't gotten picked up and tortured, Eden wouldn't have gone rogue to get him.

"So, get out of there. Take Emily out for dinner."

"Are you insane?"

"No. I think she might be there to save you from being an eejit."

"Fine."

"Good, now I have some research to work on. Go away."

With that, she hung up.

"The women in my life are a pain in the ass."

"I love you, too, Elwood."

He sighed. "Where do you want to eat?"

Another blinding smile. "Side Street Inn."

He started up the car. He knew they were all right, but something was wrong, beyond that, all of their suspects kept getting off'd, and watching the watchers usually worked for him.

He would just need another tactic, or the brewing storm would drown both him and Eden.

four

"OH, LOOK, PEOPLE TO BUG ME," Charity said as both he and Graeme walked into her lab.

Charity Callahan was the forensic genius for TFH. The African American beauty was married to their FBI liaison, TJ Callahan. She was just starting to show, which meant she must be about six or seven months pregnant. As someone who was into everything superhero and pop culture, she tended to dress as if she were going to a comic con. Today was no exception. She wore a maxi dress with what looked to be tiny Thor hammers all over it. Seeing that her husband's nickname was Hammer due to being named after the Norse superhero, it made sense.

"You know you wanted to see us," Graeme said.

She rolled her eyes. "I would if I had anything, but I have nothing."

"Are you telling me there is no forensic evidence from the murder?" Kap asked, frustration starting to brew. They were less than twenty-four hours into the investigation, and it was starting to get annoying. They knew who the victim was, but his former career had left their investigation in a mess. As usual, the CIA refused to help out with any contacts from Green's career. National Security. Assholes.

It was one of the things he hated the most about *The Company*. They put national security over everything, even the death of one of their former agents.

"Some fibers, carpet that is installed in millions of cars. It will help you nail any suspects you find, but it will not help you find them. Another thing, who said he was *former* CIA?"

Graeme and he shared a glance, then both looked back at Charity.

"What makes you think he wasn't?" Graeme asked.

"His pay. He was still getting paid by them, full pay."

"Everyone thought he left the CIA," Kap said. "Even Eden."

Her eyes widened. "Oh, wow, how was that? I forgot to ask. Pregnancy brain."

"It was fine."

She opened her mouth, probably to ask another intrusive question—as most of TFH did all the time—but Graeme interrupted her.

"So, we have a dude people say quit the CIA, but he didn't. He was here looking for your ex, who still has a target on her back."

"Wait, what?"

"You have to know whoever took her brother was never caught. Everything was very hush-hush, and I couldn't get all the information. TJ's trying, but I wouldn't hold my breath. The little bit I found indicated that both she and her brother were convinced someone from the CIA sold them out."

She let the ramifications settle over them.

"You think Green was sent here to kill her?" Graeme asked.

She shrugged. "It's a theory I have. Also, I find it odd that they haven't sent anyone in to take over the case. Most of the time, the CIA would do that for an agent."

"But everyone is saying he retired," Graeme said.

"Plausible deniability," Kap murmured.

"That's exactly what I was thinking."

"You think the CIA sent someone here to kill her?"

"Kill or threaten. I mean, it makes sense that Green would be able to get her unlisted Dillon Security number," Charity said.

Graeme's phone went off. He pulled it out and read the text.

"Dillon is ready to talk. Let's go on over and see what they have to say."

"Thanks, Charity," Kap said.

"I'll call if I find anything else, but the lack of evidence points to one organization we would all like to avoid."

The Company. Kap knew she wasn't wrong, but he'd learned a long time ago that avoiding the truth wasn't always the best plan of attack.

It took them less than twenty minutes to arrive at Dillon Security. A cute brunette with a blinding smile showed them into Luc Warner's office. Conner Dillon was nowhere to be found.

He knew the former SEAL ran the show for the most

part. Dillon was semi-retired, living on the other side of the island with his romance author wife.

"Sorry, Conner couldn't come in. He had a previous engagement he couldn't get out of. Please have a seat."

Both he and Graeme sat in the chairs in front of Warner's desk. He pulled out a few papers. "Here is an affidavit from Devon Stryker and his wife saying that Eden and El were with them when this was going on. They have included their contact information, because they both understood that they would need to talk to you personally."

"And the phone?" Graeme asked.

"Do you have a search warrant?"

"Not yet."

He sighed. "We have to wait on that, and we will not fight it. It's just we have to make sure our clients know we didn't hand it over without one. They wouldn't trust us."

He got that, but it didn't make him feel any better. Every hour that passed had his anxiety rising. Kap didn't understand why it was affecting him this way, but for some reason, he was worried more than usual about wrapping up the case.

"Have you noticed any issues in the last few weeks with Eden or El?" Kap asked.

Luc shook his head. "They only ended up working together because Mix was already booked to work security for *Task Force Honolulu*. Devon wanted a man and a woman who could work for ten days in Japan. Both she and her brother are fluent in Japanese, which made them a good fit. Also, Eden knows the Strykers."

Yeah, that made sense. There were rumors that Stryker had been trained by the CIA, and his wife was a former MI-6 agent. Kap understood that they would feel more comfortable with two former spies.

"Do you have any other questions?"

Graeme shook his head, but Kap could feel the frustration dripping from his partner's reaction. They didn't need to be dragged all the way over here just for affidavits. Those could have been sent over, which made Kap think there was more to this trip than they thought. Warner wasn't the type of man who would do a power play to show that he controlled the narrative.

"Conner wanted me to assure you that the moment you get a warrant, that phone will be yours."

"We appreciate it."

After they walked out of the building into the parking garage, he felt like he was missing something."

"That was fucking weird," Graeme said.

"Yeah. Why did we get called over?"

"It could be a situation where Conner wanted to play nice. He is always very worried about the company's image."

"Yeah, maybe. It just seemed like there was more to it."

Graeme stopped beside his SUV. "Do you think they were trying to read us again?"

Kap drew in a deep breath, then let it out. "Yeah. Which means, they don't know everything."

They both climbed into the vehicle. "So, your woman hasn't told them everything."

"She's not my woman," he said with a little too much force.

The twitch of the Scot's lips told Kap he had been screwing with him.

"You keep telling yourself that."

He decided to ignore that. "So, we think they might have been trying to figure out what we knew? I fucking hate mind games."

"Agreed, but" he said as he pulled out of the parking space, "at least we know they are worried about Eden and El."

"They think they're lying to them?"

He shrugged. "Or they just might be worried about them. Ex-CIA operative shows up dead. Makes me think they already know more, or suspect more, but they want us to figure it out without their help."

Fucking mind games.

A long shooting day had left both Ian and Eden frustrated. They had one incident with an overzealous observer, who wouldn't stop shouting their unhappiness with the scene. After that, the entire day seemed to drone on.

So, after that, she suggested picking something up and going over to her house to eat. It wasn't the first time they had done that. They tended to do it a lot when they finished a job. Most of their jobs involved around-the-clock security. Since this one had an end time every day, it made it easier.

He offered to grab dinner from L&L Drive-Inn, which was right down the street from her house. She'd tried to text her brother, but El wasn't picking up. It could mean one of many things, most of them not good. The one good thing would be that he was sleeping the day away, but she knew better. With Green's death, their investigation was getting bigger.

She arrived home and noticed that his car wasn't there. El spent most of his time on Kauai, where he had a house, so he tended to use a Dillon car when on Oahu. The calmer pace and, for some reason, the chickens seemed to keep his nightmares manageable.

Pushing her worry about her brother to the back of her mind, she decided to hurry and change her clothes. All day in her work clothes, and she was ready for some relaxation.

She was just stepping off the bottom step when there was a sharp knock at her door. After looking at her doorbell cam, she made her way to the door. Ian had a bag of food in one hand and a gym bag in the other. They all carried "go" bags in their cars. You never knew when things would go sideways.

"That smells amazing," she said, taking the L & L bag from him. "You know where the bathroom is."

He nodded and headed off to change. She'd barely eaten, even having access to the set food. Her stomach had churned all day, leaving her slightly nauseous, so she had kept her snacking light. She pulled out the containers of food, noting that he had bought an extra loco moco for her brother. Her brother, who was nowhere to be found. The one who would be royally pissed about her divulging their secrets.

But they had to trust someone. Someone other than each other and Lila/Sam. This case was spiraling out of control.

"That is damned better than wearing a suit," Ian said as he strode into her kitchen wearing a pair of shorts and a t-shirt.

"Oh, Ian, sounds like you're becoming accustomed to living in Hawai'i," she said with a smile.

"Maybe," he said, grabbing his container. "I don't know how you just slipped into life here without flinching."

Because she had lived a lie most of her life. Ian might have been raised by spies, but he had been left out of the loop until he was old enough to understand. Her family had been working with the CIA—and its precursor, the OSS—for four generations. When the world thought all you did was drill for oil, you had to put a face on it. She had become that face when she turned twenty-two, but she and El had known long before that. They had also moved around more than some military BRATS she knew.

"Goes with the embassy work my folks did for years."

"Are we eating in here?"

She waited a second or two, then made her final decision.

"No. Grab your food—did you want a drink?"

"Just water. I have a feeling this is going to be a night where alcohol isn't the best thing to have on hand."

He had no idea. They both grabbed a glass of water, then their food containers, and she led him back to her hidden room. When the door slid open, he chuckled.

"My sister would be so thrilled about this."

"Don't tell her about this. I don't want to tell you, but since you're my partner, you have a right to know."

She led him into the room, and his eyes widened when he saw all the information amassed on their boards.

"Bloody hell."

"I know, it's a bit much."

"It's freaking brilliant," he said, setting his container down before moving closer. "So all of these people are dead?"

"Yes. There were more, but these are the ones we think are the core of who were targeted."

"Motive?"

This is why she'd decided to tell him. She and El had

always worked for the CIA, but they didn't do a lot of investigative work.

"Not sure," she said.

"Then why did you zero in on them?"

"Because of the lack of motive. All of them had enemies, you can't work intelligence without acquiring some."

"True."

"But the one thing that stood out for them all was the lack of motive. Most of them did have open cases, but nothing that would have linked them together."

"Their backgrounds?"

"Some were counterterrorism, some worked in embassies."

"Like you?"

She nodded.

"Did you know any of them?"

"I knew O'Malley and Green. Interestingly enough, they were on my suspect list."

"Green died here."

"And O'Malley."

His sharp gaze cut to her. "When?"

"About four months ago. It's hard to get info on him because he was still active in the CIA."

"And you and El have been digging into these murders?"

She nodded.

"Why? What brought this about?"

She pointed to the board. "That's why. We think El was one of them."

"Okay. But don't you see what kind of danger you have put yourselves in?"

"We were already in trouble, Ian. We both had a target on our backs."

His jaw tightened. "You think both of you were targeted?"

She nodded. "There were just things that never seemed to match up. Like, how did I find out about him missing so quickly? That was sloppy for someone who spent so much time planning his abduction. It was like the bastard was trying to lure me out. I did get shot."

He opened his mouth to say something, but her phone went off. She noticed the caller ID and rolled her eyes.

Sam.

She clicked it on. "I'm a little busy right now."

"Yeah, I know Mix is there. Put me on speaker phone."

"Are you sure?"

"I think we have a red alert, and it all has to do with Elwood."

"What?"

"Dammit, just put me on speaker phone and apologize to Ian later."

With a sigh, she clicked on the speaker phone.

"Good to know you have your partner's back, Mix. I knew you would, though."

His gaze narrowed. "Sam."

"Oh, my...you sound so sexy growling my name. Does he look sexy, Ed?"

Something passed over Ian's expression. He knew that no one but El called her that. Well, it seemed that way for Sam, too.

"Stop messing with Ian. What's going on with my brother?"

"Did you know that he spent his afternoon stalking your ex?"

Alarm lanced through her. El didn't always do things like that. Oh, he would sometimes go off half-cocked, but stalking, that had never been his thing. She knew it was the PTSD, but it always worried her. "No. He did?"

"Yeah. Emily lured him away to dinner."

"Why didn't you call me?"

"I've been a little busy, so I was reviewing traffic cams around Oahu when I had a chance, and I noticed him parked there. Hopefully, TFH didn't notice."

There was something in her friend's voice that had Eden's nerves on high alert. "What are you busy with?"

"Things. Don't worry about it."

"Sam."

"I told you. Don't worry about me. Keep a tighter leash on your brother."

"Am I my brother's keeper?"

"Yeah. I mean, you always have been, haven't you? Text me if you get any information you think I need. Moving locations again."

"Okay. Be safe."

"I will. Hey, Mix, you protect Eden. She's the best person you could have as a partner."

Then the phone went dead. With a sigh, she turned off her phone.

"Okay, let me have it," she said.

"How long have you known her?"

"About five years."

"How did you know her?"

"First, I want you to understand that I didn't know she

was *your* Sam. Not until she told me. And there is only so much I can tell you."

"Her real name isn't Sam."

She shook her head.

"And you won't tell me her real name."

"No. She has her reasons, and most of them are legitimate. Some are just...well, she's a little paranoid."

"How often does she move?"

"A lot. She has reasons for that, too."

He nodded. "It's irritating that I had no idea you knew her."

"Like I said, I didn't know you two knew each other until she told me she'd checked you out and you were safe."

"Checked me out." He snorted.

"Don't discount her clearing you. She did a deep dive, and let me say that when the CIA burned her, they lost one of their best analysts. Like, ever. MI-6 tried to hire her away a lot of times before the unfortunate incident."

"What was that?"

"Her being burned. That's what she calls it."

He drew in a deep breath and released it. "So, we have a person killing CIA agents, and now your brother to control."

"Emily will be able to handle him."

"They know each other, too, I take it?"

She nodded.

"Brilliant. Hopefully, she can get him home in one piece." He looked back at the board she had up. They had spent years compiling the information, including a map that marked the locations of each kill. "I guess we should get started."

By the time Kap made it home, it was close to midnight. After a quick interview with Devon Stryker and his wife, they now knew for sure that both Eden and her brother had been off the island during the attack. And basically, they had nothing. As there were no prints, no bodily fluids, and the bullet didn't match anything in the system. So, Charity had been telling the truth.

They had fuck all to help with a CIA agent's murder.

After stepping into his apartment, he knew something was off. Then he realized the alarm hadn't beeped. He turned to look, but a voice stopped him in his tracks.

"Don't worry, Hanson. I disabled it."

He pulled out his gun before turning to find El Carlyle sitting in his living room, making himself at home. The other man turned on the table light. He was smiling at Kap, but there was nothing friendly about it.

"I think we need to have a chat."

five

KEEPING his gun trained on El, Kap walked into the room.

"What the fuck are you doing here?"

He shook his head. "I just told you, we needed to have a talk."

"You've been cleared, so why are you here?"

"I wanted to touch base with you about a few things."

"Don't worry. I won't be bothering your sister anymore."

"You'll bother her until she dies, I suspect, but I wanted to give you a little more information about the case."

"And you couldn't call me?"

"CIA, or was at one time. Don't trust phones, but according to my sister and another friend, I can trust you, so I will."

Knowing he looked like an idiot holding his gun on El, he holstered it, then crossed his arms. Holding his gun on a former CIA agent was probably stupid. "Go ahead."

"How far have you gotten into your investigation?"

Kap rolled his eyes. "You know I can't tell you anything. It's an open investigation."

"Does the name Edwin O'Malley mean anything to you?"

"Is that who you suspect?"

"No. At least not anymore. Look him up."

Then he rose to his feet. "Gotta get home, or my sister will come looking for me, and we both know she will not be happy that I came here."

"O'Malley?"

He stopped beside Kap. This close, there was no denying he was Eden's twin. They shared the same eyes. Darkness clung to him, but the eyes...they would always remind Kap of Eden.

"Yeah. I figure you can follow the footprints."

"Way not to be a creepy CIA operative."

"You forget, ex-CIA."

He headed to the front door and slipped out without another word. Dammit. Now, he knew he wasn't going to rest until he started to look into whoever O'Malley was and how he fit into the entire situation.

"Where the hell have you been?" Eden demanded the moment he walked through the front door.

"Like Sam didn't tell you," he said, letting one eyebrow rise.

"I needed you here to talk to Ian."

"Did you tell him?"

"I had to. He's former MI-6. He already knew something was up."

He grunted.

"There's moco loco in there for you. Well, the patty and rice. The eggs were gross."

"Thanks." He barely looked at her as he passed by. Alarm raced through her. This felt like it did when she'd pulled him out of that hellhole, when he had almost died. Desperation gnawed at her gut. He was shutting down again, and she couldn't have that.

"El," she said. He paused with one foot on the first step that led upstairs and looked at her. "Are you okay?"

He nodded. "It's been a long few days with the trip back from Japan." He always had an issue with jet lag. "And I know that Sam called you."

"How do you know that?"

"Because she's a busybody like my sister. Don't worry. I'm fine, Ed."

She nodded as she watched him trudge up the stairs. Worry in her gut. This whole thing was spiraling out of control, and she worried she would lose her brother for good. After he physically recovered from his torture, he was a shell of himself. Before, smiles had been easier, but even three years later, every smile he gave the world seemed to cause him pain. Eden wasn't sure he would ever be the same.

Her mind filtered back through the memories. She had been dating Kap for a month and had finally gotten permission from Uncle Marv to tell him that she was a CIA asset. While he had been an NCIS agent at the time with security clearance, her family had been different. Decades of spying for the US government had made it hard to be honest with anyone she dated. Even her best friends had no idea, except Sam, but then, she was CIA, too.

If she hadn't been so wrapped up in Kap, she would have

noticed the moment her brother disappeared, or she would have picked up that he was going down a bad road. Something.

Because, when she'd asked Sam if she was her brother's keeper, they both knew the truth was that she always had been. Eden was five minutes older than her brother. She couldn't remember a time when she wasn't looking out for him.

No, wait. It was when she was infatuated with a tall drink of water, who still got her hot whenever she saw him. Even after he turned his back on her, she'd wanted him. In her bed, in her life...but she didn't really think she could trust him. Not now with so much at stake.

"Jesus, did you go home?" Graeme asked as he stepped into Kap's office.

"I'm wearing a different outfit. And yes, I did, but I had a late-night visitor."

"I don't want to hear about any women you picked up."

"No," he said, shaking his head, exasperated with his temporary partner.

"Then who?"

"Elwood Carlyle."

"What kind of a name is Elwood?" Graeme asked.

"Probably an old family name. Anyway, he told me to look into another CIA agent by the name of Edwin O'Malley."

Graeme's eyes widened.

"I know. I was skeptical. But see, that's the thing. O'Malley was found murdered. No suspects. They are trying to play it off like it was a robbery."

"Anything missing?"

He shook his head. "And can you guess where he was killed?"

"Bugger me. Here?"

"Yeah, about four months ago. It was during the whole thing with Keely."

Keely Templeton was Ryan Morrison's fiancée. She'd been a witness to a murder, and they'd had to find her once she'd fled.

"You don't think he was trying to divert your attention."

"I wouldn't put anything past him."

He nodded.

Before he could ask Kap another question, he noticed Ian Smith walking through their common area. He shot his smile at a few people, but he had zeroed in on Kap.

"Early for you Dillon Security types, isn't it?" Graeme asked, humor in his voice.

"I'm working on the set of *Task Force Honolulu* this week. They have a night shoot, so I don't have to be in until later." His blue gaze focused on Kap. "Do you have a moment?"

"Does this have to do with the case?" Kap asked.

"Not really. It's personal."

"That's my cue to leave. I'll head down and see if Charity found anything."

He tossed a knowing look in Kap's direction. Great. Now, TFH was going to start betting on his love life.

"Come on in and shut the door," he said as he sat down behind his desk. "What's on your mind?"

Ian settled into one of the chairs in front of Kap's desk. "I want to make sure that your investigation into this Green character isn't some kind of revenge. Or at least you aren't going to use it against Eden."

Kap didn't respond right away. It was hard to hold onto his calm when his integrity had been questioned by a damned former agent.

"I would never do that."

"I know you had a relationship with her a few years ago before you abandoned her, so—"

"First, I didn't abandon her. She lied to me. I was apparently the last person to know she was CIA."

Ian cocked his head as he studied Kap. "Hmm, interesting. So much heat still."

Fuck. He was sick of mind games with spies.

"Is that all you wanted?"

"No. See, the reason Eden and I work well together is our backgrounds."

"I know you were both spies."

He shook his head. "No. We grew up in the life. Granted, I was shielded more than the Carlyles were. They lived all over the world, and knowing the two of them, they figured out at an early age that their life wasn't normal. It's not an easy life."

"Yes, living in embassies and consulates is a real tough life as a kid."

"Definitely a thorn in your side, hmm?"

"Fuck off."

His mouth kicked up, then his smirk faded. "I usually stay

out of people's personal lives, but I'm uniquely qualified to give you advice. This childhood trained her...trained me...not to trust anyone."

"I thought all spies were like that."

"To a point, but multiply that by a thousand for a kid who grew up being told they were a target. She couldn't trust a soul with her secret, and if you think back to your time together, she didn't seem to have a lot of experience with relationships, right?"

The memories he'd always tried to keep at bay came flooding back. Sending her flowers, opening doors for her...all of it seemed like it had never happened to her before. Eden hadn't been a virgin, but she seemed completely confused by his pursuit.

"Just know that you were probably her only relationship. And her situation was even more unique than mine. Her family's business had been used as a front. Any crack could put them all in danger."

He said nothing in response.

"So as long as you aren't going to bother my partner, we're cool."

"What is your interest in her?" Fuck, from the knowing look Ian just gave him, Kap had shown his interest. But he wasn't. It was just that he hated thinking someone like Ian, with his cool attitude and expensive suits—even in Hawai'i— was involved with her. And yes, he knew he sounded like an asshole.

"She's my partner. I will always have her back, no matter what. And, Hanson, remember that while I can control my reaction to your interest in Eden, Elwood wouldn't take to you breaking her heart again. And that man is living on the edge. The only thing holding him back is Eden, so be careful."

Then he left Kap alone with his thoughts.

Another long, boring day of shooting, and Eden was happy that this was their last day. Granted, it hadn't started until noon, but it was after nine now. She still had a bit of jet lag bothering her, mainly because she hadn't gotten any sleep the night before. Or, at least, not more than a few minutes here and there. She was glad she had no reason to go into the office the next day. The permanent security detail had been brought in, and they were free for other things. How did people just sit around not doing anything all day? There were a ton of people on the set doing just that. She would go insane doing that every single day.

Her plans for tomorrow involved her couch and a TV, and as many calories as she could cram into her body.

She hit the stretch of Kalaniana'ole Highway that could be desolate this time of night. Typically, it didn't bother her, but it was particularly empty tonight. She usually took Pali Highway since it was easier from Dillon Security. Still, they had finished up filming tonight in the Hawai'i Kai area, and this was just easier.

As she neared the entrance of the Makapu'u Lookout, Eden saw a flash in her rearview mirror, then a crack. Her back window shattered as someone took another shot, hitting one of her back tires.

Her car fishtailed across the road, her heart pounding out of her chest, and the world seemingly spinning as she tried to control her vehicle. She overcorrected, and her car did a complete three-sixty, leaving her dizzy. She managed to get her vehicle off the main road and onto the road that led to the lookout. Still, she slammed into the low wall that bordered the drive into the parking lot. The hit was so hard that her teeth chattered, and the airbag deployed.

Immediately, she ducked down in her car, pulling out her weapon. She was a sitting duck there, even though she knew the shooter was at least two hundred yards back.

Grabbing her phone, she called her brother, hoping he would pick up for once in his life.

He picked up on the second ring.

"Are you still on the set?"

"No. I'm at the Makapu'u Lookout."

"Kind of dark to see anything, Ed."

Jesus, her brother. "Do you think I stopped for sightseeing? Someone was taking shots at me."

"Are you hit?" He demanded.

"No. But he hit my right rear tire. I'm stuck, and I can't see anything."

"On my way."

"I'll be waiting."

"Stay safe."

"Always."

Kap pulled his SUV to a screeching stop when he reached the lookout entrance. His heart was still slamming against his ribs.

"Fuck, that was a hard stop, Hanson," Rami said. Kap didn't respond. He had been barely able to take a breath from the moment he'd heard that someone had taken a shot at Eden. He jumped out of the car and hurried over to the two vehicles parked there. He heard sirens in the distance.

He didn't care if Rami kept up with him or not. The need to see that Eden was safe overrode every instinct he had. The moment he saw her brother draping a lightweight jacket over her shoulders, Kap could finally take a full breath. For the last fifteen minutes, he had been in terror, trying to keep himself from completely losing it. As he strode up to her, anger hit him hard. She was shivering, so he did the most dumbass, manly thing he could do. He got angry.

"What the hell, Eden?"

Her eyes widened slightly. "What are you doing here?"

"I called him, Ed. He's investigating CIA agents being killed, including two here."

She slanted a look at her brother. "You told him about O'Malley?"

"And now someone is taking shots at you. We needed to report it, Ed."

"Who are you and what have you done with my twin brother?"

The sirens were getting closer.

"What is that?"

"Ambulance," Rami said.

"Oh, I don't really need that. I did get shot at, but it was no big deal."

She was trying to brazen it out. Why would she do that? It was easy to see that she was probably going into shock. Still, the stubborn woman refused to admit anything was wrong.

"How many shots?" Kap asked.

She gave him a look of disapproval, probably because he fairly growled the words.

"Two. One hit my back window, the second hit my tire."

He started counting backward from ten. If he didn't, he would definitely start yelling again. And that was not what she needed. It wasn't what any of them needed.

"Ed, I think you need to see a doctor."

She glanced at her brother. "Fine. But just the EMT." She motioned to her face. "This looks worse than it is."

As the ambulance came to a screeching halt, another car parked behind it. He knew that car, and he ground his back teeth. He knew he shouldn't be surprised that they'd called Ian. He was her partner, and Dillon wasn't going to like that one of their people had been attacked.

The former spy strode forward, a savage look on his face. Not for the first time, he wondered about their history. Both had been spies, so had it always been platonic?

Dammit. He needed to beat that stupid jealousy down. She wasn't his, not anymore. Eden had never really been his, not with the lies between them.

"Are you okay?" Ian asked her, but he thought there was more to that question. Kap knew he was letting his imagination go wild at the moment, but his nerves were already a mess.

She nodded.

"Rami, can you help Eden get to the ambulance?"

His teammate gave him a look, but he nodded.

"I can walk a few feet to the ambulance," she groused.

"Don't make me call Mom," El threatened.

She shot her brother a look, but she went off with Rami.

Kap crossed his arms over his chest and stared her brother and her partner down.

"Are you two going to tell me what's going on?"

They shared a glance that had him grinding his teeth again. Spies. They were always such a pain in the ass.

"It's Ed's story to tell," El said.

"Are you fucking kidding me? You're going to go with that?"

Before either of them could respond to his comment, his phone went off.

It was Adam.

"Be right back. Go nowhere."

Then he stomped off. Spies think they could lie to him or hide things. She was almost fucking killed, and they were still thinking they could control the issue.

"Is Eden okay?" Adam asked.

"Yeah. The EMTs are checking her out right now."

"No sign of the shooter?"

"No. It's out here by the Makapu'u Lookout. Dark as shit. I would guess he or she was up on the ridge. She said the shot came from behind."

"Okay. I'm sending out my people to look around, but you have a new assignment."

Fuck, they were going to take him off the assignment. "What?"

"You are now going to stick to her. If she's a target...you need to make sure that she stays safe."

"Got it. Her brother and partner are here."

"I wouldn't expect anything less. More than likely, they will want to handle her protection, and while I'm okay with that, and they are employed by the best on the island, I want our eyes on her."

"Okay."

"I'll call someone out for tonight, then we will also go over the scene once the sun comes up."

Rami came walking over. "Rami's here. If Eden wants to go home, he can stay here and oversee the scene."

"That will work. Make sure you keep her alive."

"You can count on that."

He hung up and looked at Rami. "Alpha's coming to handle the scene, but you're in charge until then.

"Sounds good. Your woman doesn't have a concussion."

"She's not mine."

Rami rolled his eyes and walked away to start the investigation.

Kap turned and found Eden's brother and partner staring at him. Although Adam didn't say it, he had a feeling that El was probably a target too, being a former CIA asset just like his sister.

Something niggled at the back of his brain, but he had to deal with a bunch of frowning spies. He approached them.

"Rami said the EMT said no concussion. Alpha is coming to oversee the investigation, which will be a pain in the ass at night."

El nodded. "She said the shots were from behind, so probably on that high ridge just around the bend."

Kap nodded. "And if he was professional, then he probably policed his brass, but we might find something."

All of a sudden, he heard a phone ringing and realized it

was in Eden's car. El grabbed it and made a face, but he answered.

"Marv, what do you need?"

Whoever it was, apparently answering.

"Because I did. She is indisposed right now. No, she's fine. Listen, I'm kind of busy right now, but I'll have Ed call you once she's back."

He hung up without waiting for an answer. Kap let one eyebrow rise up.

"Our old section chief. He's also a family friend."

"That you don't like."

He sighed and glanced over at his sister, who was still being looked at by the EMTs. "I never really had a problem with him, but he has an interest in my sister. It's weird. We've known him since we were like five. Gross."

Kap digested that and wanted to punch their old section chief, but again, that was irrational. Another man finding her attractive was a regular occurrence. And yes, it was gross that a man who had known her since she was a kid was apparently interested in her, but that had nothing to do with him or this investigation.

"Who was on my phone?" Eden asked.

None of them had heard her coming.

"Uncle Marv."

She frowned.

"And no, you don't need to call him. You were shot at, and you need to go home."

Her spine straightened, and he knew she was about to blast her brother. "I think I can decide where I go and when. How about you step off, El?"

"You two need to calm the hell down and find out what Kap heard from his boss," Ian said.

"Not my regular boss, but the head of Team Alpha."

"So, Adam. Just tell us what he said," Ian said.

"He wants me keeping an eye on both of you," Kap said, giving them a smile that had nothing to do with being friendly. "So, I'll be hanging around."

six

EDEN HAD her arms crossed over her chest, and she refused to talk to Kap. It was immature, and she was behaving like a temperamental nut job, but she hated losing control. She did not want Kap to know just how freaked out she was. Yes, she was a spy and had been shot once before. Most people thought spies were all like James Bond, drinking martinis and outrunning explosions. There was some of that, but she had been more of an undercover spy who worked in the open, daring people to figure out she was a spy.

And, for the most part, she had pulled it off until that one horrible weekend. Just this had her thinking about that weekend. The shot she had taken to her shoulder and the thought that she had lost her other half...her twin.

The main reason to cross her arms was to hide the fact that her hands were shaking. Hell, her entire body was shaking. Eden could always keep her cool, but once things were over, she fell apart. That was another reason she hadn't been cut out to be a spy. She hadn't had the nerve.

"Are you going to stay mad at me?"

His voice had always sent shivers down her spine. Not because she was scared, but because the man was sexy as hell. The entire package with a body built for sin, those amazing eyes, and the muscles...inwardly, she sighed. She'd always had a thing for Southern men, and Kap had a deep Georgia accent.

"I'm not mad. I'm thinking."

The sound he made told her that Kap didn't believe her. What the hell ever. She was still trying to figure out why someone would come after her. Was it because of the investigation or someone from her past? What the ever-living hell was going on?

He pulled into her driveway. Before he had it in park, she popped out of the SUV. Being cooped up with him for even less than ten minutes was too much to take. Right now, she was scared. And she wanted nothing more than to lay her head on Kap's shoulder. But she couldn't. He wasn't hers. He didn't want to be hers since he'd found out she was a dirty spy. And if she did what her brother had suggested before she'd left the scene, Kap would end up hating her even more.

"You need to trust him," El said.

She glanced at the man in question, then back at her brother. "I don't think that's important."

He stepped closer and looked at her. "You can play the ball buster with everyone else. I know you're scared. This isn't searching for some nameless asshole. This is someone who is coming after you."

"He could come after you, too."

He nodded. "I'll handle that better if I don't have to worry about you."

"I can take care of myself."

"Yeah, you can, but he's investigating the situation. Trust him."

She knew her brother was right, but she knew that the moment she told Kap, he would hate her more. And yes, she played the tough former spy, but every time he looked at her with disdain, she felt her soul shrivel.

"Hey, slow down," he said, rushing toward her. "You were shot at tonight, so don't you think I should check things out?"

"I thought maybe I shouldn't stand outside waiting for someone to shoot me from a distance."

She unlocked her front door and disabled the alarm. "See."

"Doesn't mean no one is in here."

"Dillon would have been alerted. I have a massive amount of security in the house. Cameras outside, sensors throughout the entire back yard."

One eyebrow raised. She used to love that. It was so sexy. Okay, she still liked it.

"Don't you think it's overkill?"

"Well, seeing how someone shot at me, I think I might have been onto something." They stood there, staring at each other. There was a tickle in the back of her throat. "I need a drink."

She walked into the kitchen and pulled out her bottle of whiskey. After dumping at least three fingers of it into a tumbler, she walked back to the living room. She didn't offer him any because he was on the job. Kap always played by the rules. He studied her with calm patience, as if trying to figure her out.

"Don't."

He cocked his head to the side. "Don't what?"

"Don't analyze me. You won't like what you find." Fear had her entire system working overtime to protect her, and even though she knew it was a tell, her lips twisted as she spat out, "Remember?"

Unfortunately, he didn't rise to the bait. "You aren't surprised."

She drew in a deep breath, releasing it before taking another large gulp of her drink. It would be so much easier if he would just fight her.

"Oh, believe me, I didn't have someone trying to kill me while I drove home tonight on my bingo card."

"But you knew you were being watched."

"Oh, yeah. Both El and I have been watched the last three years."

He blinked once, then tilted his head. "Does this have to do with that lost weekend?"

She let out a bark of laughter that had nothing to do with humor. "That's a good way of thinking about it. Although it was a little more than a weekend."

"Let's start there."

She took a healthy swallow, enjoying the way the whiskey burned as it slid down her throat. "I guess it couldn't hurt. The Wednesday before we were supposed to meet up, I got a call about El. He had been working in Qatar."

"For how long?"

"A couple of weeks, but he never arrived there. I didn't know. I should have known."

Not for the first time, she felt as if she had failed her brother. She had been so...infatuated with Kap that she had been slipping in her job of being her brother's keeper.

"How could you have known?"

"We're twins, Kap. We...okay, not all the time, but when we're in trouble, we know. We just know."

"Okay."

He sounded like he was dealing with a nut job, and she was sure she sounded like one. Maybe she had lost her mind over the last few years. It made sense. Now that someone had taken a shot at her, she knew that all of her suspicions were right.

"Anyway, I found out on that Wednesday—he would have been in Qatar for ten days at that point—that he was missing. I called Sam, and she helped me track him. He never made it to Qatar and, worse, there was something wrong with his orders."

"Wrong?"

She sighed. "Our supervisor never sent him to Qatar. Sam found out that he was in Saudi, so I illegally—"

"What?"

She shrugged. "It wouldn't be the first time I did that. Anyway, I slipped into the country and got him out. It took us a little bit to get back. First, he had been tortured. We found a medical facility to help in Saudi. Also, I had a gunshot wound and—"

"What the fuck?!" Kap strode to her.

"I was shot getting him out of there. It wasn't that bad."

"Where?"

"What?"

"Where were you shot?"

"Shoulder."

"And you didn't tell me."

"I would have, but you accused me of being a dirty liar

and walked away from me, Kap. What the fuck was I supposed to do?"

He opened his mouth, then snapped it shut.

"We never figured out who sent him the message about Qatar."

He just kept staring at her for a long second. "He doesn't remember his abduction?"

She shook her head. "He had a concussion, along with a broken arm, a broken finger, and two broken ribs." Eden took a quick sip of whiskey for courage. The memories always left her feeling bruised and battered. "We think that he was given some kind of drug because he remembered only stopping in to get a drink at the hotel bar in Qatar, then he woke up in a dark room. The men I took out had no identities at first, but Sam found out they were guns for hire."

"And this has to do with what is happening now?"

She nodded. "Both the men murdered here were on our suspect list."

"You still don't know for sure?"

She shook her head. "I only trust Sam and El."

"Not this Uncle Marv?"

Eden sighed even as guilt moved through her. Her parents had had Marv over to their house all the time while they were growing up, and she did look up to him. But neither Sam nor El trusted him.

"I only trust Sam and El," she repeated. "Both of them have said not to trust him."

He nodded but said nothing, continuing to stare at her. It was the longest they had spent together since she had arrived in Hawai'i months earlier. At least alone, that is. There would probably never be a time when she didn't want Kap. It was her burden.

Needing some space, she turned away from him. She only got a couple of steps away when he reached out for her. The moment his fingers wrapped around her arm, her entire body lit up like a Christmas tree. The man didn't have to do much. From the moment she'd met him, she had been overwhelmed by him. Men had always been something she could do without. Most of them bored her.

He pulled her back against him, her back to his front. He leaned down.

"I'm sorry."

Those two words almost broke her, but she kept her spine as straight as possible. At this point, she couldn't show weakness.

"It was a long time ago."

"It feels like it was just yesterday."

It did for her, too, but the last time she'd opened her heart for him, he had stabbed her and left her bleeding.

"Was this what you wanted to tell me about?"

She turned to face him. "About the case?"

"No. When we talked on the phone, you said you wanted to talk to me about something."

"You remember that?"

He chuckled, the rich sound tumbling through her entire system. The man would always be sexy. Was that why she hadn't been able to move on? She had yet to take another lover. She couldn't trust anyone, or that's what she told herself.

Was that the reason, or was the reason standing in front of her right now?

"I remember everything about you. Sometimes against my own wishes."

"I know the feeling." She sighed and finished off her whiskey. "Do you mind if I take a shower before you ask me any more questions?"

"Go ahead."

She made her way up the stairs to her bedroom. She was still shaking inside, hoping she had hidden her fear from Kap. It was her pride speaking. Still, it was all she had. Slowly, she undressed, being careful of her bruised body. Bruises always seemed to pop up hours after a wreck. Starting the water, she stepped into the shower and let the hot water relax her muscles. Still, now that she was alone, all she could hear was the crack of the shot, the flash that she had caught in the rearview mirror, and the terror that had filled her as she'd tried to save herself.

Her entire body started to shake. Even though she knew it was a delayed reaction to what happened to her, she couldn't seem to get her body to stop shaking. Leaning against the wall, she tried to get her emotions back under control. Nothing seemed to be working, so she slid down to the floor and sat there, wrapping her arms around her knees. The tears flowed, the fear leaving her a quivering mess.

"Eden?"

She registered Kap's voice, but she couldn't seem to respond. It was as if her body had shut down. Her brain was no longer working.

"Eden, if you don't answer me, I'm coming in."

She opened her mouth, but she couldn't form words. The tears kept falling. Why couldn't she speak? She needed to say something — anything at all. She couldn't let him see her like this. She was Eden freaking Carlyle, and she did not fall apart. Ever.

The door opened.

"Oh, babe," he said, grabbing a big white towel. He turned off the water, then stepped into the shower, wrapped the towel around her, and scooped her up off the floor. Instead of standing her up, he carried her to the vanity. She was thankful for that, because she wasn't sure her legs would hold her up.

"I should have known something was wrong when you didn't seem to have a reaction to the attack."

"I was trying to hide it."

He grabbed another towel and started to dry her hair. "Yeah, well, you don't have to do that with me."

Tears filled her eyes once again, and she was glad he couldn't see her this time. Tears could make Kap think she was weak, and she couldn't have that. He already thought she was a dirty spy.

But these tears weren't fear or even sadness. They were gratitude. Since her brother's abduction, she had tried to be strong. There was something broken in El, something that told her he would never be the brother he was before he had disappeared. Until the day she died, she would always feel as if she had failed him. She should have double-checked everything and ensured he was where he was supposed to be. But she had been so insanely happy she could finally tell Kap the truth.

Eden hadn't realized how much she had taken on in the last few years until this moment. The weight of it, the guilt... all of it felt as if it would bury her.

When he pulled the towel away from her head, she blinked, and a few more tears fell.

"You're breaking my heart, Eden."

"I'll pull myself together. Don't worry." She always did. It was what she did. It was what she had to do.

He cupped her face in both of his hands. Using his thumbs, he brushed away the tears. The calluses on his fingers always sent a shiver down her spine. What was it about this man? Everything about him still got to her. His looks, his work ethic, and even when he was being mean to her, she wanted him. There was something wrong with her. Something that she was sure could be fixed with a lot of therapy.

Maybe. Maybe she was just going to be in love with this stupid man for the rest of her life. And while she knew it was a mistake, and that she shouldn't give in for this one night, she needed to let go, to allow herself some pleasure. A connection. Being shot at put a lot of things into perspective.

"What is going on in that beautiful head of yours?"

She sighed as she lifted her hands to his wrists. Eden didn't care that the towel had slipped down to her lap. With Kap, she always felt bold, sure of herself. Well, until he'd walked away.

She pushed that thought aside. No worrying about what came after.

"Eden," his voice dipped even deeper. The sound of it danced over her nerve endings.

"Kapone," she said, using her Texan accent to its fullest extent. He always said it got to him.

"You should get dressed."

But he didn't move. He stood there between her legs, his thumbs now caressing her face.

"Maybe you should get undressed," she said, slipping her hands down his arms. The man had the most amazing forearms. Before she had met him, she had never thought about a man's forearms. But with Kap, she noticed everything. The way his eyes would flare when she drew out his name. His smiles. Those forearms...his stamina. The entire freaking package that made up Kapone Hanson. He was the perfect man. Or had been until he broke her heart.

Nope. Not thinking about that or anything else right now. Right now, all she wanted to do was feel. To let go of the fear that still rattled through her entire system.

He dropped his hands, setting them on either side of her hips on the vanity counter. "I don't know if this is a good idea."

She inched closer, pressing her body against his.

"It could be the worst idea in the world," she said, letting the stark honesty of the truth settle between them for a moment. "But I don't care about that. I care about feeling, about letting go of the fear that has been chasing me for too long. I know you can help with that."

He studied her for a moment, his gaze ping ponging back and forth as he studied her. That long moment was torture. She was sure he would say no and walk away again, but instead, he surprised her.

Kap bent his head. God, the man smelled amazing. Sandalwood permeated every inch of him. She had always been partial to the scent. She slid her hands up to his shoulders as she opened her mouth and gave in to the kiss.

He took his time, barely dipping into her mouth as he tilted his head. Over and over, he teased Eden in that same thoughtful manner. Her nipples hardened, her body shivered as need rose with each tempting dip into her mouth. When he finally plunged into her mouth completely, she was barely able to hold it together. She moaned against his tongue.

Kap tore his mouth away. They were both breathing heavily.

"Are you sure?"

She shook her head. "Not at all. All I know is that I need to feel something — anything. And I want to feel that with you."

With a groan, he swooped in for another long kiss, then pulled back. He scooped her off the vanity with ease and walked into the bedroom. He fairly tossed her on the bed, and she laughed. The sound of it surprised her. She didn't think she would ever be able to laugh like that again, but in this moment, she could with Kap. And that was the thing about him. Even when they were at odds, she felt comfortable with him...happier than with anyone else.

Taking hold of the bottom of his shirt, Kap stripped it off, revealing that excellent eight-pack he had. The man must work out half of his time at work, because she wasn't sure how he could maintain that muscle definition otherwise. She reached out to explore.

His hands went to the button on his pants, then stilled.

"Fuck."

Her eyes shot up to his face. Even in the darkness, she could see the irritation. Exactly what a woman didn't like to see from her lover.

"I get it. Just go," she said, humiliation filling her once again. When would she learn with this man? He was just never going to be hers again, even for one night...one little last tryst.

"No. I just don't have any protection with me."

For a second...okay, three...she wasn't sure she'd heard him right. Then, happiness filled her, starting with a slow trickle, then a monsoon swept through her.

"I'm on the pill, and I'm clean."

Of course, she was. There had been no one since him.

"I'm clean, I promise."

"Then I suggest getting those pants off, Kap, because this is much more fun when we're both naked."

"You trust me?"

She didn't look away from his earnest expression. She heard the seriousness of his tone and knew what he was asking. It was bigger than just a tumble in bed.

"Always."

Something akin to surprise sparked in his eyes before it was replaced with heat. He reached for her hips and pulled her to the edge of the bed.

"You're still dressed," she said.

"Well, it's that or I'll lose control. First, it's time for you."

Then he dropped to his knees between her legs. This man...he had been the one lover she could trust over the years, and, even with their past, she still did. She knew that at least in this moment, she could trust him. He would be careful with her...and he always put her first.

He leaned forward, pressing his mouth against her right thigh, his tongue tracing a path almost all the way to her pussy, but he stopped short. He moved to her other thigh, starting at the top, and gave it the same treatment. Then, he dragged the flat of his tongue up her thigh once more. Every inch or so, she felt the scrape of his teeth. Heat filled her, her sex growing wetter by the second. It had been so long since she'd felt like this, of letting go and giving into pleasure.

She felt his breath a second before she felt his mouth on her sex. He didn't hurry. He rarely did in bed. Oh, there had been some quickies, but when Kap was trying to prove a point, he didn't rush. Taking his time, he slipped his tongue inside of her, teasing her with each dip into her core.

"Kap."

He hummed against her, the vibrations filtering throughout her body. Heat spiraled, her entire being centered on him and what he was doing to her. Fingers replaced his tongue as he took her clit into his mouth. The tension in her stomach spiraled, then dropped lower. He pulled back to blow on her clit, then he was on her again.

Her orgasm hit her so hard, it was almost violent. She bowed up on the bed, screaming his name. Wave after wave of pleasure rolled over her, through her...

It lasted so long she felt suspended in time. It had been too long since he had touched her, since any man had touched her. This felt almost like coming home.

She was still feeling the aftereffects of her release when he stood to peel off his pants. He flipped her over on her stomach, and she laughed in joy. He remembered that this was one of her favorite positions.

He pulled her hips up and entered her in one hard, long thrust. Their mingled groans filled the room, and it was possibly the most erotic thing she had ever heard in her life.

"Fuck, Eden. So. Fucking. Good."

He thrust in with each word, sending more sensations rushing through her. The man always knew how to play her body. From the moment they'd met, they had always seemed to understand each other's needs.

Even though she thought it might be impossible, she felt that familiar tension building again, and Eden wanted to be with him this time around. Slipping her hand down between her legs, she pressed against her clit, thrumming it.

"Yes, that's it, babe, make yourself come. I want to feel all those tiny muscles tighten around my dick."

His deep voice sent her rushing over that edge, as she jumped into a morass of pleasure once again, her world seemingly exploding around her.

"Fuck!" he said, thrusting harder and faster than ever before. His fingers dug into her hips as he raced over her, until he thrust one last time.

"Eden," he said as he emptied himself inside of her. His orgasm seemed to go on forever before he finally pulled out of her.

She seemed to float for a moment or two, then she felt his hands on her again. He was turning her over and using a wet rag between her legs. She should protest, but she felt too good to even contemplate words. Then, he was moving her up to the pillows.

"Are you leaving?" she asked.

"No. Be right back."

He returned from the bathroom and slipped into bed beside her. And just like all those times before, she rolled over into his arms.

"Get some rest. We'll worry about the rest later."

And because she agreed, she slipped into sleep.

seven

IAN WATCHED El pace the living room floor. His partner was going to owe him for this one. Her brother was a live wire, ready to explode.

"I don't know why I'm here. I should be with Ed."

"Yeah, well, she asked me to look after you."

"I'm not a toddler."

"Could have fooled me," he murmured.

El stopped and looked at him. "She trusts you, so you get some trust from me, but not blind trust."

"Back at ya."

The former spy frowned at him. "Did you ever work in the Middle East?"

He shook his head. "I was more Europe and Russia, so we didn't cross paths. I still would have pegged you for CIA, though."

"What's that mean?"

"You know. The way you handle yourself. The constant looking for exits, always wanting to have a way out of the room. The hyper vigilance."

"That could mean we were just military."

"Ah, but...you never had time in the military. You both spent time in the Middle East with a wealthy Texas family that often resided there. I would have known you were like me."

El studied Ian for a long moment. "Yeah. We are alike. Your dad was MI-6."

"And my mother. We go a long way back as spies for the crown."

"But you moved to Hawai'i."

"My sister was here doing things that could have gotten her killed. *Almost* got her killed. So, even in that, we are alike."

He rolled his shoulders. "I'm the reason she's at risk."

"She's at risk because of her birth. You were born into the situation you're in."

He nodded.

"How do you feel about Kap?"

"Hanson?" El asked.

"Yeah. I have a feeling that guy is going to want to be in her life again."

"Not sure he has that choice. Ed...she could have handled anything, but when he walked away from her, he broke her."

"Ah, spoken like a man who has never been in love."

"And you have?"

"God, no. But I watched Seth almost lose Autumn."

El frowned, then headed over to look out the windows. They were in Ian's condo, which looked out over the Honolulu Harbor. His and Autumn's father lived in Kailua, and he spent a lot of time over there. Tonight, though, he thought it best to stay in the city. While his father was a former spy, he didn't want to entangle him in this mess.

"I just don't like any of this. Other than you, we are all back in circling. Me, Ed, and Hanson."

"Let's start there. I looked at your research."

"Mainly Sam's research. She's a fiend, always has been about research." His voice had softened ever so slightly, and Ian ground his teeth. He didn't like that at all. He had no idea why her friendship with El mattered, but it did.

"You know her well."

He nodded. "Best damned analyst the CIA has ever had. Those idiots didn't know what they lost until they burned her. I'm sure someone is trying to figure out a way to bring her back."

"How did she get burned?"

He sighed. "One of the reasons was that she was helping us. Or that's what Ed and I think, at least. The person responsible for killing all the agents must be fairly high up in the organization. He or she would have to have the resources and the connections to commit all those killings."

He digested that. "Either way, we need to take a step back and look at this investigation."

"That's why I need to be out there."

"No. Taking a step back means taking a break. Let your mind rest."

He opened his mouth, but Ian held up his hand.

"I know. Don't you think I recognize the guilt? Dad had plenty of that after he found out about Autumn. He had no idea he had a daughter, but when he found out that she had been stuck in that hellhole of a cult for her entire life, he had to work through all the guilt. So, I get it. But you or your sister shouldn't feel guilty."

He tossed a look at Ian over his shoulder. "You think Ed feels guilty?"

"Yeah. Eden thinks she let you down."

"She didn't. I let myself down."

El turned back to look out the window, and Ian rolled his eyes. These two were such martyrs.

"Get over yourself. You need to get out of the way, or both of you could end up dead."

He whirled around to face Ian. "I know that. I didn't think the bastard would go after Ed. If I did, I would have made her go back to Texas."

He snorted. "I've been partners with your sister for almost six months. She would not have gone back."

El shook his head but said nothing.

"Since it seems neither of us is getting any sleep, why don't we go over the case?"

"We could do this at my sister's house."

Ian remembered the look on Kap's face, the way he seemed to twitch every time someone made a comment about how close Eden had come to being hurt. He was sure the former NCIS agent was about to pull his head out of his ass and claim his woman. That was something a brother should never experience.

"Why don't you call Sam so we can go over some of these cases. I've been doing a little look—"

"Oh, Ed is not going to be happy about that."

"Well, I'm not particularly happy with some git taking shots at my partner."

El studied him for a long moment, then nodded. "Let's get to work."

"Call up Sam and let me run some things by her."

"You don't have her number?"

"No, I don't. She calls me from all kinds of numbers, which I am sure she's doing to protect her position."

"Probably," he said, pulling out his phone. "Probably also trying to protect you."

He blinked. "What?"

"She doesn't want you to have the knowledge of where she is so that people don't think they can get it from you."

"But you know."

"Well, Mix, thanks to Ed and me, she's been on the run for years now. So, I figure she assumes we have it coming."

He clicked on his phone and switched it to the speaker. He hit a saved contact.

"I'm not happy with you," she said, her husky voice filling the room.

"First, not my fault. I can't follow Eden around. And second, you're on speaker."

"Oh, goodie. What up, Mix?"

"How did you know he was at my place?"

She snorted. Right, she was a genius at tech.

"Ian has some ideas on our victims and thought we should run them by you."

She made a small humming noise, and the tapping of keys reached him. "Good. Let's get to work."

When his phone rang in the middle of the night, he knew it was going to be bad news. It was an instinct that he'd had for decades and one that he kept him alive.

"Yes?"

They never used names when they talked on the phone. He knew he was running circles around the office. All those lazy bastards who couldn't handle the jobs they had been handed.

"No luck tonight."

He let the silence stretch out. The fucker had cost him a pretty penny, and he couldn't get the job done. This is why he had been the one to kill the others. Hiring other people to abduct or track his quarry had been easy. He couldn't be seen in those locations all the time, so it worked well to have others do the footwork.

The killing...that had been his. This was the first time he had hired someone to actually kill one of his targets, but he knew that Eden, El, and the rest of their motley crew were getting too close to the truth.

Killing Eden had been on his agenda this early in the game, but he'd realized the act would send dear old El spiraling. They were going to be his last kills before he disappeared with all the money he'd acquired.

"That is not the news I wanted to hear."

"It was a bitch of a shot, and she was late tonight."

"I don't take kindly to excuses."

"I can get her tomorrow."

Probably not, but that wasn't important at the moment.

"Tell you what, you go retrieve her and keep her contained."

"I'm not a kidnapper."

The dumbass said the word "kidnapper" like it was beneath him. He was a hired hitman. These idiots.

"Unless you want me to make sure that everyone in your line of business knows you didn't get your mark…"

He let the implication simmer. Men like this Jackson bastard were only successful because of their reputation. One little slip-up didn't just hurt the business. It could ultimately lead to his death.

"Fine. I'll get her at her house."

"Good. I'll be there by morning. Let me know where you're keeping her before I land."

He hung up without another word. He had no reason to tell that man that failing would end up in his death. Jackson had signed his own death warrant the moment he missed killing Eden.

Rising from his bed, he started to make plans. He had one more loose end to cut off before he headed to Hawai'i.

eight

"THE RUSTLE of sheets forced Kap to open his eyes. He hadn't felt this relaxed in three years. It took his brain a second to catch up to where he was, why he felt so good, and the fact that Eden was slipping out of bed.

"Where are you going?"

She smiled at him over her shoulder. Her hair was a bit of a mess from his hands and had been left damp. Even in the dark, he could see the scar on her shoulder. The bullet wound he hadn't known about when she had come to see him. Even thinking about someone shooting her made him want to strangle the person who did it.

"I didn't want to wake you."

He sat up. "We need to talk more."

Her smile faded and she nodded. "Come on. I'll show you everything we have."

"Everything?"

"Yes."

She slipped out of bed and grabbed a pair of sleep shorts

and a tank top. After Kap pulled on his cargo pants, he followed her into the bathroom.

"God, my hair," she said with a sigh. "This is why I have to blow-dry it out. Hawai'i doesn't like my hair."

He watched as she tried to tame it. It was a mass of curls he had never known she had. It was sexy and, even as she tried to comb it out, the curls suited her. It also revealed more about her personality to him.

"You're a control freak."

She glanced at him. "I just like things a certain way."

He snorted as he crossed his arms over his chest. Kap wasn't ashamed to admit he liked the way she seemed momentarily distracted by the movement.

"That's the textbook definition of a control freak."

Those clear blue eyes narrowed as she studied him. "Excuse me?"

He chuckled. "You wouldn't use that tone with me if you knew what it did to me."

There was a long pause.

"What *does* it do to you?"

Her voice had dipped lower, and she licked her bottom lip. Of course, his unruly dick hardened. It had always been like this with her. There had been a few women since they had dated, but they had never captured him like she had. The memory of every moment had been imprinted on his soul, and he couldn't seem to move on.

"Stop that. We have work to do right now."

"And later?"

"Up to you."

Her eyes sparkled as her lips tipped up. It was the first genuine smile he had seen from her in years. From the moment he'd run into her here on the island, she had seemed...not sad, but not happy. Something was weighing her down, keeping her trapped in some way.

"Let's go look at this research you have," he said, hating the way her happiness seemed to fade. The sooner they got to work and figured this out, the sooner...his mind had been moving in a direction that he hadn't planned. After their breakup, he had convinced himself that he didn't need her. But now, even when they were sparring and she was calling him "Kappy," he felt more alive than he had since they had been together.

Pushing those thoughts aside, he followed her down the stairs to the wall in the living room. She hit a button, and a door slid open.

"Could you be more of a spy?"

She snorted. "This was here when I bought the house. It is one of the reasons I bought it."

She stepped into the small room, and he realized it was some kind of panic room. The lights came on automatically.

The entire wall was filled with an investigation that must have taken...

He glanced at her. "How long have you been working on this?"

"Since my brother and I have completely recovered. We knew there was something more than the CIA wanted to admit."

He nodded as he looked over the research and the connections they'd made. Kap knew she had been a CIA agent, but she wasn't an investigator. She probably could have worked at the BAU with this level of work. The list of abductions, ten to be exact. Nine deaths. One survivor.

"You could have let this go."

"No. I couldn't."

He glanced at Eden. Her arms were crossed, her expression determined.

"You think whoever it is will come after your brother?"

"First, if we hadn't found the others, we probably would have let it go. Or at least hired someone else to deal with it. But these are agents. All of them are dead for some reason we can't figure out. There is no connection with their work."

"They're agents. They had to have some enemies."

She made a rude sound. "Yes, but if you look closer, every one of them was considered not because of the job."

"Don't they cover up their deaths? The CIA lies about things like that, right?"

"Yes, to the public."

It took a second for the ramifications to sink in. "You've seen the official reports?"

She nodded.

"How?"

"Can you arrest me if I know someone who hacked into the CIA and made copies?"

"You know someone who can hack into the CIA?"

"No comment."

He growled. "I won't arrest you. You didn't do it."

"Then, yes, I do know someone who can hack into the CIA."

He shook his head. "Charity will be very jealous of that ability."

"She's tried to hack into the CIA?"

Kap shrugged. "I know that she can hack into several

organizations, but she's never mentioned the CIA. So, the official story about El?"

"He was captured by terrorists, and the one thing he remembered is that they spoke English. *American* English. They were not from the Middle East, as the CIA is claiming. That's what set off our alarm bells."

"Does anyone outside of you and El know about this investigation?"

She hesitated, and he felt his temper flare to life. She was still trying to hide things from him.

"Don't look at me like that. I won't give up the hacker's name without permission."

He blinked.

"But Ian knows. I had to tell him a day ago because his spy senses were on red alert, and he knew something was going on."

Her phone rang and she rolled her eyes. She answered even though it had to be about three in the morning.

"What do you have?"

Maybe the hacker. She glanced at Kap. "Are you sure?"

Some more talking from her friend.

"Okay." She clicked the button for the speaker. "Kap, I believe you know Sam."

"Sam? The one Mix hates?"

"Only because I kick his arse seven days a week and twice on Sundays. Nice to have you on Team Catch the Bastard."

"Quit with that name. We both told you weeks ago we were not going to use it. What did you find?"

"Well, I just chatted with your brother and the man who loses to me every week—"

"Sam."

A sigh. "Fine. I just wanted to let you know that I am going to look at connections between the victims. I will start with you and El since I know your life story well."

"You don't think it was some American group?"

"You know I'm convinced that it is tied to one person in the US. If I do another deep dive into these people and find something that matches with you and El, we might find a string to follow."

"Why haven't we done this before?"

"We have. But you were left out of the equation. I want to look at why someone would come after all of you."

"We all had prices on our heads."

That had alarm racing through Kap. "What?"

She looked at him and shrugged. "Goes with the territory. Although the price on our heads is gone. We have no connection to the CIA anymore. Since my family is no longer privy to information, we aren't high on anyone's list. Our inside information is old and useless."

"That's what Mix said. We were listing all the things you had in common with the victims, and, of course, we reviewed your work. But you and El really didn't investigate. You moved information, kept an eye on things at the consulates and embassies. Your family has never been one of those who engaged."

Kap had been thinking the same thing earlier. "So you think it is something on a personal level?"

"Yes. I'm sorry, I didn't think about it before."

"Don't. You and I know that you have spent years poring over the details. We looked into their personal lives."

"But not enough. There has to be something that

connects all of you. If it isn't the job, then it is something in your background."

"And the hit on her last night?"

"That is the anomaly. I am going to do some research on an idea I have."

"Sam," Eden said, worry threading that one syllable. He looked over at her.

"No, I'll be careful. Don't really need to hack anything. I know I have something that connects all of you in some way."

"You could have called me tomorrow about this. Why now?"

"Well. Your brother was very excited, and I was worried that maybe you and the very handsome Officer Hanson might be indisposed."

Eden's face flamed, and Kap chuckled.

"Do you need any help from Charity?" Kap asked.

"No. I got this. It's all the files I came up with on my own. I need to sit with them and look. I know something is there."

"Thanks for the call."

"No problem."

Then the line went dead.

"She's not good with normal human interaction."

"You know this, Sam? She's the one who helped us when Jin and then when Autumn was in trouble."

She nodded. "El and I have known her for years."

"Do you know why she's on the run?"

She nodded, sadness filling her expression. "She helped me find El against orders. She wasn't directly ordered not to, but she was aware of the rules. Then, she started poking around for us on her own. She knew we were getting frustrated, so she jumped at the chance to help. I know we aren't the only reason. When she began searching for information for us, she discovered something else. Not sure what it was, but our actions caused her to find something that sent her into hiding."

Kap now had a better picture of what was going on and why Eden felt the weight of the world on her shoulders. Guilt was the cloak that dampened her shine. He had thought he was seeing the true Eden months ago when they ran into each other for the first time. Instead, he thought he might have it backwards. Now, she hid her feelings, and he hated that he was part of the reason why.

"Hey," he said, taking her hand and pulling her into his embrace. It seemed like the most natural thing to do. For three years, he had been trying to get her out of his system, but none of that had worked. And now, he could see why. He understood on a level that maybe he hadn't been ready for all those years ago. "We'll figure it out."

She pulled back enough to look at him. "We?"

"Woman, I'm not about to leave you hanging. Even if this wasn't my case, I would help you."

"Don't be nice to me, Kap. I can't handle it." Her tone had turned brittle. It was as if he said one word wrong, she would fall apart.

"Well, get used to it, Eden."

She swallowed. "Just...don't be nice to me for the investigation. I can handle anything but your being nice."

"You want me to be mean to you?" he asked.

"I can't handle you being nice to me, then not."

Understanding slammed into him. He had wounded her more than he had known, and it was his own damned fault. His fucking ego had been damaged. Kap had struck out, fear being the main reason. In the following years, he had convinced himself that he had been right. That she had lied to him made her untrustworthy. Now, he understood more, and maybe, just maybe, he'd never get her to trust him again. Panic clutched him by the balls at that thought.

"I know I was an ass before, but I promise not to turn my back on you. We are in this to catch the killer."

She nodded, then settled her head against his chest again. He just had to figure out a way to prove to her that he had learned from his dumbass mistakes from three years ago.

They heard a car door, and she sighed. "That has to be my brother."

But before they could get to the door, alarms were going off.

She frowned and looked at her doorbell app. She held her phone up for him to see. He saw two people wearing ski masks—not common in Hawai'i, of course. Then, they reached up and hit the light.

"That is not my brother," she said.

Fuck, he'd left his gun upstairs. From the look on Eden's face, she had the same thought. "Do you have Graeme's number?"

She shook her head and, of course, he didn't remember it.

"I'll call Ian. He'll get hold of them."

She moved further back in the safe room as Kap shut and locked the door. Usually, he would confront the guys, but since they had come armed, it was best to wait for reinforcements. On top of that, he had no idea if they were alone. It went against every instinct he had. He was a fighter and a protector, but he knew it could get them both killed.

"Ian, are you on your way here?" She listened to him for a

second or two. "Get your ass in gear. Two intruders are in my house." She rolled her eyes. "We're in the safe room. Hurry."

She hung up the phone, then brought up another camera. Kap crowded closer. It was a camera from outside showing that there was one driver in the car. With her brother and Ian on the way, they should be fine.

They listened as the bastards stomped up the stairs. "Eden, you might as well come out now."

That helped clarify what these two wanted. They had not hit her house randomly.

More stomping around, things breaking, and now they were getting frantic.

Kap pulled her closer, and she shivered in his embrace. He didn't know if she was freaking out or if she was angry. Perhaps a mix of both, but likely more anger. The murmur of voices faded as they headed out of the house. Soon, they heard the sound of El and Ian calling their names.

Eden unlocked the door and stepped out.

"Ed!" El said as he rushed toward her, pulling her into a big bear hug. It only took a moment for him to take notice of Kap standing in the doorway. His gaze moved down Kap's body, and by the time he'd raised his eyes to meet Kap's once again, there was anger simmering in them.

"What the fuck?"

"It's the middle of the night," Ian said, tossing Kap a bone. "Besides, we have more to worry about if someone was looking for your sister."

"Exactly," she said, pushing away from El and stepping closer to Kap. "We need to figure out who the hell they are and just what the hell they wanted."

And they needed to do it before the bastards came back.

"We need to move you," Ian said. "This place isn't safe."

She nodded, and her shoulders drooped a little. Kap wanted to pull her into his arms and tell her everything was going to be all right, but, at the moment, he wasn't sure if she wanted that from him, especially in front of her brother and partner.

With a sigh, she rolled her shoulders, then her spine straightened. "I'll go pack a bag."

Once she left, El stepped closer to Kap. They were close to the same height, but Kap had a few pounds on the man. Kap understood that El was probably more lethal than he had ever been.

"Just so you know, we will be having a discussion about whatever is going on here."

"Calm down, Elwood," Ian said as he started looking over the lists. "First, it's the middle of the night, so it's to be expected that he is half-dressed. But secondly, your sister is a grown woman. She makes her own mistakes without your interference."

Both he and El were locked in a stare-down.

"There has to be something that connects all these people." The murmur was barely above a whisper, but it reached both him and El. They turned to look at the other man.

"We talked to Sam before the men showed up. She said there had to be something, and we needed to start with both El and now Eden."

"Why Eden? I was the one taken."

He looked at Eden's brother. "Because they're coming after her now. Granted, it might be because you're stirring up trouble, but I don't think it is." He also had been thinking about this—although it left his blood cold. Three years ago, El had been taken, but the breadcrumbs to find him didn't seem that difficult. "Also, she was told of your abduction. That might have been about getting you and her in the same place to kill you both."

"Agreed. There has to be something that connects all of you," Ian said.

"You should call Sam," he said to El. "We need her to see if she can trace the men who were here tonight. They didn't seem to be that good."

"They got the drop on you."

"Actually, they didn't. We were down here looking these over when we heard them drive up. We had no weapons on us, and they came in hot."

"Fine, but we will be having a talk."

He said nothing to that as El turned away and stomped out of the room.

"You will have to deal with him, you know."

"Nothing happened." But his voice did not sound convincing to his own ears.

"I'll call Dillon and get a safe house."

"Wait," he said. "I think we need to go with a TFH one."

He glanced up from his phone to look at Kap with one eyebrow raised.

"Y'all had your information compromised already."

"Do you think you have a better place for her to stay?"

"We need something not on the record. Do we know of anything that would work? Nikki has some connections, but they're mainly on Maui. I know Eden doesn't want to go there."

"Indeed. Let me put a call in to Warner. He might have some ideas."

"Do you trust him?"

He studied Kap for a long moment, his gaze assessing. "With my life. And better yet, I would trust him with my sister's life."

Kap nodded.

"Then do it. This bastard seems to be ramping things up. We need to get them both somewhere safe."

nine

THEY WENT to TFH headquarters first. Eden was exhausted but keyed up. She'd already had a bit of an adrenaline crash, but she was wired up again. The building was quiet when they drove up, and her nerves were on edge. She knew the men who showed up at her house had been hired hands. They hadn't been the people who were after all the agents for the past four years.

It didn't mean that those people wouldn't have been standing outside waiting for them. The hairs on the back of her neck stood on end, telling her that they were being watched.

As they walked in, she was surprised to see the activity in the common room. A considerable chunk of Team Alpha was there, and it looked like all of Team Bravo was there, including Ryan Morrison and his SARS partner Maya. She had heard he was on the mainland visiting family.

"So," Autumn said, stepping forward, "I hear you had visitors. Sam told me she's hunting them through the traffic cams. Charity tried to come in, but we have Sam working until a decent hour. Then Charity will take over."

Eden nodded. She and Sam had been texting. "Thanks."

Autumn studied her for a long moment. "You look better with your crazy hair."

Then she looked at Kap. "Glad you aren't dead. Gotta get a snack."

Eden blinked and looked at Kap. He shrugged. "You know what she's like."

"I don't like my crazy hair."

"I think it's sexy," he said.

"Ugh, stop," El said. "I don't want to have to beat the crap out of you."

Kap rolled his eyes.

Adam came striding out with Graeme on his heels. "Ms. Carlyle, you haven't been as forthcoming as you should have been."

She sighed. "I'm sorry, but I was worried about putting anyone else in danger."

"Bullshit. You thought there could be a leak, so you didn't trust us."

Adam wasn't usually so blunt. She felt Kap bristle next to her, but Eden didn't want him getting in trouble for insubordination. "Okay. That too."

"Well, at least you're being honest."

Before she could respond to that, the front doors opened. Eden blinked. Emma Delano came striding into the room. Del's wife was a certifiable genius. As in, gaming companies and government agencies hired her regularly. Eden knew that Emma sometimes helped with TFH investigations, and that was how she had met Del.

"I hear we have patterns to look at," she said.

"Yeah," Kap said. "Do we have the information set up for Emma to look over?"

"Yeah," Drew said, rising out of his chair and hitting a few things on his tablet. A screen on the wall came to life, displaying all of Eden's research. "Sam sent us all the info you had."

"Okay, I need some caffeine, and then I will get to work."

Seth came out and nodded to her. "We have the personnel files for everyone up there, but I think we need more info."

"Wait, how did you get those?"

"Sam sent them."

"You and El need to sit down and go over them," Adam said. "There might be something there that clicks with you both. Something that we might overlook."

"Like what?"

"Their files don't have the gossip. And I know there is always gossip—among other things—that happens at the office that might not make it into the files. You and El might think of something."

She nodded. That was actually an excellent idea.

"You can use conference room B."

Once she and El were settled, Kap seemed to linger for a moment before saying, "I'll be in the common room."

Then he slipped out of the room. It was stupid to feel deflated. It wasn't like they were back together or that he would stay with her, but it didn't mean she didn't yearn for that.

"Oh, stop mooning over him," her brother said, disgust dripping from his voice.

"Get bent, El."

"I don't get it."

"What do you mean?"

"He broke you three years ago."

Anger raced through her blood. She didn't usually have a quick temper, but she was exhausted and stressed.

"He did not. I was not broken."

She said it with such vehemence that her brother's head snapped up. "You were. You cried, Ed. You never cry over a man."

"Wrong. I cried over Tad."

He made a face. He had never liked her high school boyfriend. In fact, now that she thought about it, he didn't like any of the men she'd dated. Was that why she had never let him meet Kap?

She pushed that thought aside.

"You take the first three and I'll take the next. Think of everything you heard about them through gossip, even unsubstantiated."

He looked like he wanted to say more, but instead, he nodded. They worked in silence for a while. The only sound was the scratching of their pens as they made notes and the turning of pages in the notebooks they were writing in. They could always do this, even when they were kids. They had that weird twin connection that even if they were irritating the hell out of each other, they liked to be close. Codependent? Yep, but with their childhood as the children of CIA operatives, they could only trust each other.

"Why did you cry over that asshole?"

"I was sixteen and he broke my soft heart," she said, sarcasm dripped from every word.

"And your head? Is it screwed on straight?"

"Has it ever been?"

His eyes narrowed. "Ed, I just want to make sure..."

She sighed and reached across the table to take his hand. They had been through hell together these last three years. "I'm good. Don't worry about me."

He turned his hand so his palm was facing up, and he could grab her hand. "But I do. They never...they never came after you before."

"But what if they did?"

He let go of her hand. "What?"

"What if they used you to lure me out?"

He closed his eyes. "Ian was thinking the same thing, which means you got shot on purpose."

"Of course I did. That was no accident," she said, humor lacing her voice.

He opened his eyes, regret shimmering. "Don't joke."

"Hey," she said, getting up from her chair and going over to him. "We have to joke so we don't fall apart. You know that. But either way, I think they wanted both of us."

He frowned up at her. "Both of us?"

She nodded. "I think they took you because you were the one going around to other sites."

One of his jobs for Carlyle was PR. He would go around and drum up business for their company, but he would also do a little work for the CIA. She had done the same thing up until the year before his abduction.

"It could have been me."

He sighed. "If you say so."

He had never been so pessimistic, but forty-eight hours in hell could really fuck a person up.

"I do. So, that might help us. Let's keep working on these

lists. I want everything you can think of, too. We both knew a lot of the same people, but we also had different relationships. Plus, men are gossipier."

"I take offense to that," Ian said, walking into the room. She rolled her eyes.

"Give me a break. Y'all are always worse than we are. Including at Dillon. I have never heard so much illicit gossip from Emily, and you know how much she talks."

He chuckled. "That is pretty bad. Are you coming up with anything?"

"Not yet. We're still just going through and listing everything."

"Okay. I'll be back in a bit."

"Where are you going?"

"I want to stop in to talk to Warner, keep him updated."

She nodded. All of them were trying their best not to use electronic devices. All three of them never trusted the safety of that. The spy business had taught them that nothing electronic was ever really safe.

As if her phone had been privy to her thoughts, it vibrated on the table.

"Who is it?" Ian asked. "If it's Sam—"

"No." She looked at her brother. "It's Uncle Marv."

"Marvin Bellows?"

She nodded.

"You need to take it," El said.

"Why?" Usually, her brother didn't want her to tell Marvin anything. It wasn't that El didn't trust him in particular. Marv was still with the CIA, and El would never trust anyone who was still working with *the Company* again.

"You might be able to get information from him. It isn't like he's the sharpest tool."

That was true. He had risen through the ranks, stepping on other people. As much as she loved him like an uncle, he was also kind of an ass. Working for him had been fine for her, but she knew a lot of other people didn't like him.

The phone stopped vibrating.

"Seriously, you need to call him back." She kept staring at her brother, waiting for his reasoning. "He might call Mom and Dad."

"Shit. Yeah."

She picked up her phone and hit Marv's contact number.

"Eden, it's so good to hear from you. I was worried."

"Why would you be worried?"

"I heard there was a shooting in Hawai'i."

She blinked as she looked first at her brother, then at Ian.

"There are shootings here all the time, Marv."

"Hold on a second."

She heard him move, and it sounded like he was shutting a door. This was something he didn't want anyone else to hear.

"There are rumors."

"What rumors?"

"First, a blond woman who works for Dillon was shot last night."

"Well, I wasn't shot."

She wasn't shot, only shot at. If she could keep as close to the truth as possible, she would convince Marv. And why was she doing that? One reason was her parents. As bad as the situation was, adding them to the mix was a bad thing. They would not just ruffle feathers. They would pluck those feathers brutally.

Marv sighed, relief filling his voice. Unlike her brother, she trusted their old family friend—to a point. He was still a company man, and she knew that if anything went sideways, Marv would side with the CIA. It was his life. He had no kids, no wife, nothing outside of his career.

"That's good to hear. My next call was going to be to your parents, although I didn't want to do that."

"Well, I'm glad you didn't warn them. Was there something else?"

"What?'

"You said there were a couple of reasons why you called. Was there something else?"

"Oh, yeah. Listen, I'm glad that you and El landed on your feet with Dillon."

"Thanks. We like working for Conner. He's been a great boss."

She put a little more emphasis on the word boss for a reason. There was no reason on Earth that Conner would leave them behind. Warner was a former SEAL, so she knew the two of them would never abandon their agents. Marv had done just that. It was CIA protocol to deny everything. They knew that going in, but she had never thought he would do that to them. Naive? Yes, but he had always been a part of the family.

"I just want to talk to you about your partner."

"Ian?"

Ian's eyes narrowed as he studied her. She was thankful she had decided not to put the phone on speaker. The former MI-6 agent was usually very chill, but the anger she saw in his gaze told her that he would have probably lost it if he had heard this discussion first-hand.

"Yeah, I've been checking him out."

That had her blinking.

"Why would you worry about him?"

"You know, I think of you and El as part of my family."

"I understand, but Dillon hires only the best."

There was a pause. "That's what I understood Green was there doing."

"Oh, was he? TFH stopped by to ask me about him, but they didn't say what he was doing on the island."

"Everyone I talked to told me that he was there for an interview."

"If he had one, I have no idea," she said, lying easily. "But then, El and I were off the island for a job."

"Oh, okay. Well, now that I know you're okay, I need to get back to work."

"Thanks for checking in."

She hung up. "That was hella weird."

"What?" El asked.

"It was like he was fishing for information. What do we know about David Scott?"

"Who is that?" Ian asked. "And don't think you're getting off that easily. I will want to know what he said about me."

"David Scott is Marv's supervisor."

"And to answer your question, I don't know much about him," El said. "The dude is paranoid."

"He was up on your board as one of your suspects," Ian said. "Do you think he's using Marv to get information?"

"He could be."

"You call him Uncle Marv, but he's not a relation?"

She nodded. "Mom and he came up through the ranks of the CIA together. He doesn't have much family, and he's never been married or had kids."

"You think he would actually sell you out?"

"Definitely," El said. "His whole life is his career. He would do anything—and I mean anything—to get ahead."

Ian looked between the two of them. "There's a history."

Not a question. "Yep. He wouldn't help me find El. Protocol," she said, not able to hide her disgust. "I didn't ask for an op, just a location. He refused to help, saying he was trying to save my career."

"And that's why you had to call Sam," El said quietly. "This caused her entire life to fall apart."

"She would kick your ass if she could hear you right now."

El snorted, then he sobered. "Yeah, he might be considered family, but that job is his top priority. If David sent him out to find information, he would do it."

"Now, what did he have to say about me?"

She sighed, suddenly feeling her lack of sleep. "He said not to trust you. That he'd had you checked out and that there were bad things about you."

Ian's face went blank. "I see."

"But he doesn't know we're still in contact with Sam," she said. "Which tells me whoever is feeding him information must be using that connection in more ways than one."

"You mean that Scott might be telling him that Ian is a danger to you? Or possibly Dillon as a whole?"

"You know he was upset by not giving me the information I needed to find you. He didn't show it much, but I know it did."

"So, you have your former boss's boss trying to get him to isolate you?" Ian said. "It's not completely insane, but it still needs information to back it up."

"I think if we can find out what these people have in common, we will be able to pinpoint who wanted them dead. The only other suspect we have is Gary Collins."

Ian sighed and nodded. "I'm going to go talk to Dillon and set up a safe house for you."

"I thought we were going to use the TFH one?"

She hated the idea of not staying at her home. Throughout her years in the CIA, she had never felt a connection to a place like Hawai'i—not even in Texas, where her parents lived. She adored her house and her neighbors.

"I figured it might be better to have more than one ready."

"Thanks, Ian."

"I'll walk you out," El said.

"You are not leaving me with all of this, El. It doesn't work without you."

"I'll be back."

"I'm a big boy," Ian said as El walked behind him out of TFH headquarters. "I can get to my car on my own."

The morning air hit him as they walked out to the parking lot. Hawai'i could be muggy in the morning, but he knew the afternoon heat would burn the humidity off. Honolulu was just now waking up, and rush hour hadn't gotten started just yet. El loved this time of day, especially in Hawai'i.

"I wanted to talk to you about Marv."

"I know you don't like him."

"Yeah."

"I don't like him either."

"You know him?"

"No. But I know the type. They would sell out anyone to get ahead. Plus, he was trying to drive a wedge between me and Eden. That makes me suspicious."

"He is such a yes man that Ed is probably right about why he did it."

"But?"

He sighed as they stopped next to Ian's car. He had been suspicious of Ian when his sister first started as his partner. Once Sam had checked him out, and El had gotten to know him, he'd begun to like the guy. He was intelligent, dependable, and not as stuffy as he sounded half the time. It was that public school British accent of his.

"You're right. He would sell me out. He would sell Eden out. Granted, he wouldn't go ahead with it without getting something in return, but he would still get it done."

"He sold you out when you were taken," Ian said.

"No, not in the way you think. You know what being an operative means. You get taken, especially in a powder keg environment like the Middle East, and *The Company* will deny knowing who you are. Going in, you understand that."

"Your sister didn't stick with that plan."

His mouth curved. "My sister would never leave anyone behind."

"That's good to know."

"So, on some level, she understands what he did. She would never be that person, but she gives him some grace because I think she feels sorry for him."

"How so?"

"He has given his entire life to the CIA. The man has no family. Not even any siblings. His parents died when he was in college. He never married."

"So, pity?"

He smiled. "Yeah. That's the basis of it. And while I don't think he had anything to do with what happened to me or what is happening now, he can't be trusted."

Ian nodded. "I'll reach out to a few people I trust about him. First stop will be with my father. He knows everyone on both sides of the Atlantic."

Ian's father had been MI-6 also. He might be able to give them some insight. "Be careful. One thing we know about these assholes is that they monitor things we're doing."

"Sure thing."

Then, he slipped into his car and pulled away from TFH. El was heading back into the building when Team Bravo, sans Kap, came striding out of the building. He didn't know much about each member other than Kap, but he knew that they were considered the SAR group.

"Where are y'all heading?"

"We're headed over to the sniper's nest," Seth said. "Did you want to come?"

He hadn't expected that.

"I would love to, but my sister and I need to keep going over all the victims. We're the two with insider knowledge."

Seth nodded, and they went on their way. He wanted to go with them. To be doing things rather than sitting around.

He knew he was needed by her and, for once, he would definitely prove he had his sister's back. As he walked back into the building, he realized that part of him still blamed himself for what had happened. He knew that whoever was behind this was a master manipulator. He wasn't the only agent who had fallen for the lies that had almost ended his life. His question had always been, why had he been left to live? So many of the others were found in less than twenty-four hours after they went missing. He had been kept alive.

"Hey," Ed said as he walked back into the room. He stared at her. "What's wrong?"

"Something that has bothered me."

"A lot of this crap bothers me."

He sighed. "Why did they keep me alive?"

"That's a good question," Ed said. "But the others—"

"They were all found within twenty-four hours. Why was I kept alive? Even Don Simmons, who was the first, was found dead within twelve hours. Why did they keep me alive?"

Her face seemed to lose color.

"What?" he asked, almost afraid of the answer.

She swallowed. "Me."

"What?"

"The one thing they could count on would be that I would look for you."

He didn't want her to be right, but in his heart—worse in his gut—he knew she was. And if she was, he hadn't been the only target three years ago. Someone had either used him to lure her out or had wanted them both dead.

ten

BY THE TIME they arrived at the safe house, Kap could tell Eden was exhausted. Not that she would ever admit it to him. Instead, she had that spine of steel and laser focus like always.

They had decided to split her brother and her up. El had gone to a Dillon Security safe house, and TFH was taking care of Eden. There had been no way that Kap would have let her out of his sight. He was starting to worry that he wasn't going to be able to let her go.

Graeme parked the SUV in front of the house as the other TFH SUV slid into the spot beside them. Kap had always liked this house for its security. It was built into the mountain, so there was only one way in, and it was easy to keep whoever they were hiding safe.

Adam and Tamilya from TFH Alpha went into the house. From their security, they knew it was safe, but TFH didn't screw around with people's safety. They triple checked everything.

Kap glanced at Eden again. This woman...fuck. She was a puzzle, one that he would always want to solve. He knew it was definitely the wrong time for those kinds of thoughts, but he was beginning to realize he was still in love with her.

After all these years, he was finally admitting to himself that she had him wrapped around her little finger. Worse, he knew he would be happy to be there. He would take all of the baggage that came with her as long as he could have her.

"I'm not going to fall apart, Kap. I can handle this."

He didn't doubt that. Her voice was quiet but determined. The person hunting the twins had probably made the biggest mistake of their life. This woman wasn't going to let it go until she made sure the bastard was dead.

"I know that."

She finally glanced at him. Then after a long moment, she nodded in acknowledgment.

The light on the front lanai blinked on and off, giving them the all clear. With that, they headed into the house, grabbing their bags out of the back of the SUV. Once the door was shut behind them, he pulled in a deep, cleansing breath.

"That seemed easy enough," Adam said.

"Almost too easy," Tamilya said.

"I agree, but who knows what's going on right now. Did the bastard who shot at me actually do the shooting? Or did he hire someone for that?" Eden asked.

"Why would that matter?" Kap asked.

"If he or she were a hire, like contracted, there's a good chance there will be another attempt soon."

"And if not?"

"The person will lie low and try when our guard is down." She sighed. "Which room do you want me in?"

One thing about Eden was that she understood how they worked protection.

The Team Alpha members stared at Kap, as if willing him to take the lead.

"Top of the stairs, to the left. There's a master bedroom."

She nodded and trudged toward the stairs. She paused. "Thank you, everyone. I don't know what El and I would have done without the help of TFH."

Then she ascended the stairs. He watched her go, his heart breaking with each step she took. It wasn't until that moment that he realized just how worried she was about the whole situation.

"That is one tough lady," Adam said.

He nodded and looked at the Alpha Team leader. "You have no idea."

"So, are you going to pretend that you two aren't back together?" Adam asked.

"We aren't together."

Did he want that? He was starting to realize that he definitely wanted that. He wanted her in his life, in his bed. Hell, he had only been with one woman since they'd split, and that had been a drunken night of trying to forget the woman who owned his heart.

One woman.

Fuck. He was definitely still in love with Eden. He loved her smile, the way she gave him shit, and he loved that she would show her vulnerabilities to him. He had a feeling she didn't do that with many people, even her brother.

Tamilya stepped up beside him. "Hey, you might want to go up there."

He glanced at her. She was a stunning woman. Tall,

athletic, and an expert on terrorism, she'd joined the team after it had been formed. She and her husband, Marcus—the captain of the newly formed Team Charlie—had had a relationship years earlier. Kap didn't know the entire story, but he knew that they found their way back to each other.

"I thought she would need some space."

She shook her head. "Believe me, she wants space from us, but not from you."

Tamilya's voice dripped with experience, and if anyone understood what was going on right now with Eden, it was probably Tamilya. She might not know Eden well, but her relationship with Marcus gave her intimate experience to provide the advice.

Ignoring the other two men, Kap made his way up the stairs two at a time. Urgency filled his gut. There was something in the way that Tamilya told him she would need him, that she thought Eden would want to see him.

He found her sitting on the bed, staring off into space.

"Eden?"

She blinked and looked at him. It was like watching a scene in slow motion. Then, she was a flurry of action. Popping up off the mattress, she started babbling.

"Sorry, really tired. Need to get in the shower."

"Eden."

"I take it we're all secure?"

She didn't look at him as she unzipped her suitcase. In fact, she avoided making eye contact.

"Eden."

Still moving. Still not looking at him.

"Of course, we're all secure. I mean, TFH is a good organization. Not as good as Dillon Security, but then, what can you do? You don't have the resources that we do."

"Eden," he said, stepping forward. He wrapped his fingers around her wrist as gently as possible. If she had wanted to break free, she could have done so.

She stood with her head down, apparently interested in the floor.

"Are you going to look at me?"

"I can't."

"Why?"

She sighed. "I brought this problem to your door and now you're having to deal with it."

"It's my job."

She shook her head. "I can handle things like this. I was trained for it."

He knew that she was trying to convince herself, but it still angered him. Not particularly at her. Anger at the situation and her upbringing. Kap kept thinking about what Ian had said. Being raised like she had, she'd probably always felt she needed to control every situation. There was a fair amount of his heart breaking for the woman...the young girl she had been. He heard the recrimination in her voice, and it was directed solely at herself. Eden thought she had failed in some way.

"Eden."

"I don't want to be a bother."

"Woman, you are going to bother me until the day I die."

Her head snapped up before she tried to twist away from him. Her cheeks had flushed with anger. Good. That was better than her looking like she was on her deathbed.

"Well, rest assured, I will be out of your life as soon as we find this bastard. Also, I can get another bodyguard. I'm sure there is someone at TFH or Dillon who can protect me."

"No fucking way."

She blinked. He didn't cuss much, but he couldn't stop the anger that whipped through him at the thought of someone else taking care of her needs. He knew that it was probably a better idea because his heart was involved. Still, even if someone took over her protection, he wasn't leaving.

He pulled her closer. "You seem to think that bothering me is a bad thing, but I'll let you in on a little secret. I will want you until the day I die. I have wanted you every day since the day I walked away like an asshole."

Her mouth opened, then closed. Kap liked that. For once, she was starting to understand what she meant to him—even if he was just beginning to understand it himself.

"Do you know that there has not been another woman since you?"

She shook her head. "You slept with Amy Miller."

Of course, she knew that. The woman was a spy. He should have known that she would have kept tabs on him.

"I was very drunk, and I was hurting."

"Sure."

Her tone told him that she didn't believe him. "One night. One freaking night that I was missing you, thinking about you, wishing things had been different. But I was angry and, being a typical man. I couldn't admit I had been wrong. I knew you couldn't tell me you were an operative. My brain knew that, at least."

"Then why did you say those things? Why did you leave me?"

Her eyes shimmered with tears, and that broke his heart.

She had always presented herself as this strong woman who could handle anything, and she could. Kap had no doubt about that. Eden was ten times stronger than he would ever be. But...she was human, and he had broken something between them.

"Ego."

She rolled her eyes, then brushed away the tears with her free hand.

"Eden, you have to understand. I knew that we had something special, but..." He hesitated for only a second, but it was enough for her doubts to take hold.

"Never mind, Kap. When this is all over, we'll avoid each other again. It's a small island, but I'm sure we can figure out a way."

Again, she tried to twist away and step around him, but he stopped her.

"I was fucking scared."

She stopped moving.

He didn't take his gaze from hers. "I was a coward. I knew I was falling in love with you, so that fear made me lash out at you. I was a dumbass."

"You were."

Of course, she wasn't going to deny that, and he didn't think she should. Still, it stung.

"If I had found out before you left, if you had told me, I am not sure what I would have done. My reaction might have been different, but my pride was hurt, and I took it out on you." He swallowed and tried his best to steady his nerves.

"I was going to tell you that weekend."

Her whispered confession hit him straight in the heart with a dagger. Three years, and each day, he had convinced himself that he didn't want to be around her. He had been lying.

"There has been no one else. Not here," he said, pressing his hand against his chest. "And after that one stupid night, there has been no one else."

She blinked. "Don't lie to me, Kap. I never expected you to stay away from women."

He shook his head.

"No. People talk. Dillon Security has too many connections with TFH. I know you have a reputation."

His mouth curved. "I cultivated that. I never wanted them to know that I was still hung up on a blue-eyed spy who wrecked my world."

Her face crumpled.

Panic hit his system. "What?"

"I ruined everything. I couldn't tell you right off, but I wanted to. For the first time in my life, I wanted to share my entire life with someone."

He pulled her closer, wrapping his arms around her. "I would like that."

She pulled back and looked up at him. She was not a pretty crier. Her skin was so fair that it turned her face all blotchy.

"Kap," she whispered his name, and it was his undoing.

He bent his head to take her mouth, and she met him halfway. She slipped her arms up his shoulders, pressing her soft body against him, and he gave in to his needs. His cock hardened, his entire body vibrating with the need he had for this one woman. This one little waif, whom he knew could probably kill a person with her hands. Why did that turn him on even more?

He pushed that thought aside as he slipped his hands down her body to her ass. He lifted her against him, and she wrapped her legs around his waist. Even through their clothes, he could feel her heat. The memory of having all that wet warmth surrounding his dick almost had him coming in his pants.

He set her down on the bed, breaking the kiss so he could tear off his shirt. Her hands were on his buckle, undoing his pants.

"Eden."

She smiled up at him, her eyes dancing with happiness. And in that one moment, he would deny her nothing. He wanted to make her smile like that for the rest of their lives. That thought should scare him, but instead, it gave him peace. They had a lot to work out, but he knew that he wanted to be by her side.

Pushing that thought away, he focused on what she was doing. She had his pants undone and was slipping her hand in to pull out his cock. Slipping her hand down the shaft, she pumped him once, twice...a small pearl of precum wet the head. Eden licked her lips, then leaned forward to take him into her mouth. He curled his toes into the rug as she licked him from balls to tip, then took him into her mouth completely. Her hand slipped down to his ball sac, teasing him.

Over and over, she took him, and it took his entire concentration not to come. He looked down at her bent head, and just the sight of his dick disappearing into her mouth had him growling.

"Enough," he said as he pulled her back. She pouted up at him, and Jesus, that almost had him coming. What the fuck?

This woman was undoing him with just a pout. It was just like before, but somehow better.

"I like being in charge."

He chuckled. "I know you do, and I'm cool with that, but I want both of us naked and enjoying it."

"But I do enjoy tasting you," she said, smacking her lips together. God, this woman.

"Naked or no more tasting."

"Fine."

They both pulled off their clothes in record time. He lay down on the bed.

"Come on, babe," he said, urging her to straddle him. "Now scoot on up here for me."

"I thought you said I was going to be in charge?"

"You will be, but before you ride me, I want to make sure that you are ready for my cock."

She shivered, causing that wet pussy to glide over his dick. He ground his teeth together. When she positioned herself over his mouth, he slipped his hands to her ass once again and feasted.

The taste of her had always been amazing. Hot and spicy, with just enough sweetness to make it addictive. Eden had always been responsive to him, as if one touch from him turned her on.

"Yes, fuck, Kap. God."

Her moans weren't exactly quiet, and he didn't care. He couldn't give a fuck what was going on outside of that room. All he cared about was this woman and bringing her pleasure. Her juices were wetting his face, and he knew she was close. Instead of pushing her to that pinnacle, he released her.

Eden looked down at him, her breasts rising and falling

with each deep breath. She had never been that big, but those breasts...he loved them. The pink nipples, the way he could palm them, and they were so fucking responsive.

"Your turn to take charge," he said, his voice deeper than before, his arousal easy to hear.

Her blue eyes were so dark, but need flared. She scooted down his body so that she was straddling his hips. Taking his cock into her hands, she stroked him once, then positioned her core directly over the tip.

Inch by inch, she descended on him. She definitely took her time, biting her lip as she tortured him. By the time he was fully seated inside of her, he was ready to come. There was no way on earth he was going to climax without her. He wanted her with him, so he held back, his fingers clawing at the bedsheets before he slipped them up to her breasts.

Plucking at her nipples, he enjoyed the way her pussy spasmed around his dick. She had always loved to have him tease her breasts.

"I want a taste, babe."

He wasn't above begging, but she took pity on him. Leaning forward, she braced her hands on the pillows as he rose to take one nipple into his mouth. His fingers continued to pinch the other, and Eden never stopped moving. Over and over, with a few twists of her hips, she rode the fuck out of him.

Soon, he knew he couldn't hold back anymore.

"Are you close?" she asked, rising up away from him again. Her rhythm seemed to double. Her hair was a mass of shiny curls and a mess from his hands. Her entire body was flushed with arousal, and she was riding him with wild abandon.

There had never been a more beautiful woman. Not for him.

"So fucking close. You always know how to ride my dick."

She moaned at his dirty words, and he could tell she was close too. So, he slipped his hands down her body to tease her clit. One press and she slammed down on him, her entire body shaking with her release.

"Kap," she moaned. Fuck. So beautiful.

He took hold of her hips and thrust up into her twice. His orgasm exploded from him, his entire body going rigid as he lost himself to pleasure.

After a speedy shower that resulted in another quick and fast bout of lovemaking, they collapsed in bed. Eden knew she shouldn't feel so happy. In fact, everything that was going on should scare the hell out of her, but in the moment, she wanted to savor this man.

They were lying in bed, wrapped around each other, her head on his chest.

"You said you were going to tell me the weekend you disappeared?"

"We call it the lost weekend."

He was trailing his fingers up and down her arm. The easy affection in that move made her want to dance with happiness. They still had a lot to deal with. Someone wanted her dead, and possibly her brother, for some unknown reason. Kap had run at the first sign of a problem, but she felt that now they might be able to talk it out. Not right at this moment. First, the bastard killing agents needed to be brought down. Then maybe...

"So, you were going to tell me?"

She lifted up off his chest, resting her weight on her elbows. "Yes. I had to get it approved."

"Approved?"

A sigh escaped before she could stop it. She would rather snuggle in bed and not ever leave. Still, she knew they had to deal with this situation.

"Even though we were not top-notch agents, we still had to get approval as to who was told about our involvement."

"What do you mean, not top-notch?"

"We weren't considered real agents. We were more assets, although we trained as agents."

His gaze narrowed. "Why?"

"Why were we trained?"

He nodded.

"Well, Mom was an agent before she met Dad. She said that if we were going to continue helping the US government, they would train us to protect ourselves."

"So, you had to tell someone? Get approval to tell me?"

She nodded, unsure where he was going with this line of questioning, but she was starting to see that he was putting some kind of puzzle together.

"Who knew?"

She blinked. "Well, El."

"Okay, I get that your brother knew."

"And my parents knew about you."

"You told your parents about me?"

"Yes."

He digested that. "But workwise, who knew? You said you needed to get it approved, so who did you tell?"

"Oh. Well, Uncle Marv, who would have sent it up the ladder for approval. You had an extensive record with NCIS and top security clearance. So it only took a week to get approval. How did you find out? That I was with the CIA?"

"Word came through another agent."

"CIA?"

He shook his head. "Amy."

She bit her lip as she started putting the pieces together herself. "Someone knew about the two of us, and the fact that Amy was hot for you."

"She wasn't—"

"Kapone, she practically jumped you when we broke up. They used her."

"Yeah."

"And don't feel guilty. She put my entire world in jeopardy by leaking the information. She knew that my family could become targets the moment she let it out who we were. She didn't care."

"Yeah, well, either way, we can't ask her who told her because she's dead."

She blinked, realizing that they hadn't even thought about who might have told Kap. They should have.

"How?"

"She transferred back to the States after I told her that I wasn't interested in a relationship. A car accident. Bad weather."

Or, she had help.

"Who did you think sold you out to the press?"

She shrugged. "Marv tried to tell me it was you. I knew

better. You would never do that to me, no matter how pissed you were. Above all else, you wouldn't do that because of national security."

He said nothing, and she looked at him. "What?"

"The fact that you believed in me when I didn't give you the same courtesy. Kind of makes me feel like an ass."

She smiled. "You weren't the one lying."

"You were doing your job. My ego was in overdrive trying to convince myself that you were bad because I was falling for you, and it scared the shit out of me."

"What?"

He leaned forward and brushed his mouth over hers. "I was falling for you, still am if you want to know that truth."

Before she could answer him, there was pounding on the door.

"Come on, love birds. We have information," Graeme called out.

"That Scot has lousy timing." He gave her a quick kiss on the mouth before he rose out of bed. He was pulling on his pants, and she was still trying to wrap her head around the fact that he said he was falling for her.

"Kap."

He paused as he grabbed his shirt off the floor.

"What's wrong?"

She wanted to tell him that she never stopped loving him. That in the last three years, she had tried to get herself free of the hold he had over her. That he hurt her so badly, and she should never forgive him, but she couldn't. Not now with everything on the line.

"Listen, I want to talk all of this out, but with this bastard out there, we need to take every lead as fast as we can.

I feel that we're close, so we get this done, then we talk it out."

She smiled. "I'll hold you to that."

"I'm counting on it."

Once she got dressed, they hurried downstairs. The TV screen was on, and she recognized Emma Delano and Team Alpha member Drew Franklin. She knew he was helping out when Charity needed breaks.

"So, what do we have?" she asked.

"We're waiting on your brother to show up on screen. We thought it best to wait until you were, you know...not disheveled," Tamilya said under her breath.

She said nothing to that. Eden and El were more than twins. They had been teammates, working together as assets. They were best friends.

Another window opened. Her brother and Seth popped up on the screen together.

"Oh, good. Finally. I felt like this was taking forever," Emma said.

"What do you have?" Eden asked.

"We have a connection among all the victims. Well, several connections. First, we discovered something odd about you all. Did you know that all of you had family members in the CIA?"

"No. I mean, I knew about Green's uncle," El said.

"Yeah, he would brag about it all the time," Eden said.

"Well, all of you had some kind of connection, either through parents, grandparents, or, in Green's case, an uncle or aunt." "Sam."

"Who?" Emma asked.

"Sam. She had a father and a mother. So maybe we

weren't the reason she was burned," Eden said, looking at her brother.

"Could be."

"Well, we can sort that out later," Emma said. "Another thing that we found for all of you, including both you and your brother."

This woman was killing her with her dramatic pauses. "What?"

"Every single one of you had a price on your head."

"Are you saying that there was a hit on each of us?"

"Yep. And both you and Elwood have active hits on you right now."

"It's been on us that long? Three years?"

"No," Emma said. "This hit was put on you just in the last three months."

eleven

WAITING to return to TFH until the next morning just about killed Eden. She was ready to get out there and kick some ass, although she didn't know which way to go. Kap had done his best to distract her with another multiple orgasm event, and she only got a few hours of sleep.

Her eyes were still gritty by the time they got to TFH headquarters. She might have her head held high and look like she was ready for a fight, but truthfully, she was tired. Tired of this asshole who wanted to hurt her, hurt her brother...and tired of pretending that she was a strong person. She wasn't. She was an imposter.

That was the worst part of it all. She and El had the same training, and she excelled at her job at Dillon, but she was never more than an asset to the CIA. El had been the one who went out on missions. He had put his life on the line, while she had hosted parties and socialized at embassies and consulates.

When they stepped into the common room, it was a hub

of activity. Team Alpha and Bravo had assembled, along with a couple of people she didn't recognize.

"Your bosses are here," Kap murmured, nodding to Del's office.

She glanced over, and her shoulders drooped. Warner and Dillon were there, and her heart sank. Maybe they would choose to let her and El go because they were too much of a problem. Having two of your agents targeted by a nut job would probably not be good for business.

"What's wrong?"

She looked at Kap. "Nothing's wrong."

One eyebrow raised in question, and, dammit, that was sexy. Whatever he saw when he looked at her had him grabbing her hand.

"Give us a sec, guys. We'll be right back."

"Wait, where's my brother?"

"He just pulled into the parking lot," Drew said.

She nodded, then let Kap drag her away. Once in his office, he shut the door, released her hand, and leaned back against the door.

"Are you blocking me from leaving?"

He shook his head.

"Then what do you want?"

"I want you to tell me what the hell is going on?"

"What the hell does that mean?"

"Eden."

She said nothing because she felt her nerves fraying, as if they would come all unbound and she would start blubbering. She couldn't do that. It was a weakness she had, one that she had beaten out of herself. Showing emotion on the job.

"Babe."

If any other man had used that term with her, she would have kicked him in the nuts. Kap had told her once that he had never used it with another woman, and she had believed him. He was good. He wasn't a dirty spy who lied.

"You've got me worried. Tell me."

She shoved a hand through her hair. "I'm worried they will fire El and me since we've created this big mess."

"First, if they fired you over this, they are dumbasses. And one thing I know about those two men, they aren't dumbasses."

"No, they aren't."

He leaned forward to take her hand. With gentle ease, he tugged her into his arms. "And this isn't your fault. This bastard is the root of the problem, not you and not El."

She knew it was indulgent, but she snuggled in closer and drew a deep breath. Kap always smelled of crisp, clean air and something deeper, masculine. When they had been dating, she thought it was cologne, but she soon realized it was just Kap.

"That's not all you were thinking about there."

Dammit. He had always been able to read her, since the first.

"I'm not an agent."

"I know that. I mean, I know you don't work for *The Company* anymore."

With a sigh, she leaned back to look at him. "No. I was never an agent. I had the training, but I was never in the field like El. I was hosting parties and meetings and basically playing spy."

She waited for a response, but he said nothing. Kap revealed nothing as he studied her, and she couldn't take it anymore. Breaking away from him, she walked away to look at the pictures he had on the wall. But she didn't see them. Not really. Instead, she realized her entire world was breaking apart because she knew at this point, he would walk away.

"Can you explain something for me?"

"I'll try," she said, without turning around.

"Did you have training like a typical spy?"

She nodded. "Mom insisted. She said that we were going to be put in danger, so she wanted us to at least have the background to deal with it."

"Who went after El?"

Turning to face him, she blinked against the burning in her eyes. She was trying very hard not to be a blubbering idiot, like she had been the night before. "I did."

He took one step, closing the distance between the two of them.

"That seems like something an agent would do. You saved his life."

"Of course I did. He is my brother and was my partner at the time. I would never leave my partner behind."

"And I'm sure the higher-ups wanted you to leave it alone. Once caught, CIA agents are usually SOL." *Shit out of luck.*

She nodded.

"But you went. With no support. Would you do that for Ian?"

"Of course. I just said I would never leave my partner."

"One thing I've noticed about you is the way you hold your body."

She blinked at the switch in topics.

"Okay?"

"And you're leaner. Not skinnier, leaner with more muscle. Let me guess, training for Dillon?"

She nodded.

He slipped his arm around her waist and pulled her against him. "And me? Would you come and save me?"

There was a seriousness in his question, something beneath it that had her heart beating so hard she was amazed he didn't hear it.

"Eden?"

"I would come for you and beat the hell out of whoever had the nerve to touch you."

His mouth twitched. "Being known as an agent, or feeling like you are one, isn't as important as that. Loyalty... true loyalty is a rare thing. Whether you felt like an agent then or now isn't as important as that. Lots of people with training would balk at saving their partners. Most people would go with the CIA rules and say they couldn't do it. When it counted, you rose to the moment. Don't ever forget that."

A lump rose in her throat, and she found it hard to swallow. Their affair had been intense, but Eden had never heard this kind of passion from Kap before. In fact, she wasn't sure she had ever heard this kind of passion from another person. He meant every word, and her heart was singing as happiness trickled through her. The dread she was feeling was still there, but this helped alleviate it.

"Thank you."

His mouth curved. "I will be happy to remind you whenever you need me to."

She lay her head on his chest, soaking in his warmth and his acceptance. Three years ago, he had broken her, but now, she understood that she should have fought him. Bonked him in the head or something to prove to him that she was not the person he thought she was.

And he had been honest last night. He had made sure that she understood that his reasoning wasn't sound, but he owned up to it. She had to give him the same explanation, but there was a knock at the door. Their discussion would have to wait.

"Come in," Kap said, not letting go of her.

The door opened. "Hey, the dudes from Dillon want to talk to you," Autumn said.

Eden peeked around Kap and found the Alpha Team member eating, of course. It was really sickening that the woman seemed to eat enough for a village but never appeared to gain any weight.

She nodded. "Thanks. I'll be right out."

When she left, she didn't close the door, and Kap rolled his eyes.

"Don't worry, Kap. But I promise, we will have a serious discussion about us after all of this is done."

"I look forward to it."

They walked out, and all the talking in the common room stopped. Again, Kap rolled his eyes, but Eden just laughed. She noticed her brother was in with Conner and Warner.

"I better go see what they want."

"You need me, just let me know."

"Always." Then she rose to her toes and brushed her mouth over his. There were whispers behind her, but she didn't acknowledge them. Instead, she just walked to the office.

She knocked, then opened the door when Del waved her in.

"Eden, we've been updating both Dillon and Warner."

El stood. "Where were you?"

"Talking to Kap about something."

"Is that a euphemism for sex?" he asked, disgust dripping from his voice, but there was a thread of humor in it. She knew he was trying to settle her nerves.

"Get bent." She looked at the other men. "What have you told them so far?"

"We know that you two have been stalked across the world," Conner said.

"We didn't know."

They both opened their mouths, but she held up her hand. She might have second-guessed doing that before her discussion with Kap, but the truth is that the little talk had boosted her confidence.

"You knew about El being abducted and that I went after him. You knew about his injuries and about mine. It wasn't like I was hiding anything from either of you. And we thought that whoever took him was finished with him. We have no insider information on ongoing operations. The threat was deemed over by the CIA."

Warner gave her a nod. So that was good to know. He was in their court. He had been a SEAL and understood a lot of what the two of them had been through. Rumor was that the managing partner of this Dillon branch had been captured and tortured while he'd been active duty.

On the other hand, Conner had been a top FBI agent. While his job had been dangerous, he hadn't been through what the three of them had.

"And now?"

She shrugged as she looked at her brother, then back at

Conner. "I have no idea. I can't understand why we're still on a list, unless someone is after us for a different reason. Emma is one of the smartest people on the planet, so I would assume that her connections are correct."

As if on cue, her phone buzzed. She pulled it out of her pocket.

> Sam: Emma's right. I'm sorry for missing that.

After Emma had dropped her bombshell, Eden had texted Sam, who had started to dig in.

> Eden: Don't. We all missed it.

> Sam: We have another problem. Marv is missing.

"What's wrong?" El asked as he stood.

"Marv is missing."

She started thinking back to her last weeks working as an asset. There had been some resistance to her relationship with Kap due to Marv's boss, David Scott. And now, as they drew closer, Marv disappears?

"That would be Marvin Bellows?" Del asked.

She nodded. "Sam is saying he left work yesterday, and no one has seen him since. His car was found abandoned on a back road in Prince William County."

She kept reading the messages from her friend.

"Anything else?" Conner asked, his voice intense.

> Sam: Phone found, damaged, Marv nowhere to be found.

She raised her gaze to El's. "He's missing, phone left behind. This isn't good."

"Would someone use him to get you to come out?" Del asked.

She looked at the TFH Commander. "Yeah. He's a family friend. We call him Uncle Marv. He knew my mother before she met our father, so our relationship with him started before birth."

"Is there an APB out for him?"

She shook her head. "Not sure."

"Well, we'll handle that."

"Thank you."

He nodded as he headed out the door.

"How are you two holding up?" Conner asked.

This is why she worked for Dillon. He could be a hard ass and a bit of a Boy Scout about rules, but he always had their backs.

"Fine," El said. "It's been a pain being moved around, but other than that, it's been okay."

"We are going to figure this out," Conner said.

She nodded, even as an impending sense of doom weighed down on her. It felt as if there was a massive clock ticking away, counting down to the next murder. She sent a prayer up that no one else was hurt before they could catch the bastard.

Kap was rolling his shoulders, trying his best to rid himself of the energy that had built up. It was annoying not to be doing anything. This was the one part of the job that he hated. Even when he was with NCIS, he hated waiting around. Of course, there was an added layer of irritation because he knew this was killing Eden.

She had been in direct contact with Sam for the last hour on and off. They were both hunting down leads but coming up with nothing. Marv Bellows was still missing, and he knew that weighed heavily on her as well.

He watched as she paced back and forth on the far side of the room, talking to Sam.

"She'll be fine," her brother said from behind Kap.

Kap turned to look at the man. "I know that. Your sister is the strongest woman I know, besides my mother, of course."

His mouth twitched. "Yeah. Us Southern boys and our mamas." His smile dissolved. "She's always been the stronger of the two of us. No matter how many times I tell her that, she doesn't believe me."

"Those forty-eight hours..."

He sighed. "I knew she would come for me. Even in the worst of it, I knew that my sister would find me. And in that, I could go on. If I didn't have her, I probably would have told them everything."

"Naw, you wouldn't have."

"Why do you say that?"

"Because you have the same DNA as that woman. You're right, she's stronger than both of us, like most women. But even knowing you have backup, a lot of people give in to torture right away. And I know that you were both trained to be agents, but you were never meant to be, am I right?"

He nodded.

"I've heard of agents that gave over info right away."

"I'm still puzzled about why they kept me alive. I know they were trying to get her there, but they didn't have to keep me alive for that."

That had been bothering Kap as well. The twins seemed to be the exception to the rules, which was worrisome. It was as if whoever was in charge treated them differently. With a bastard like this, that wasn't a good thing.

"We have another problem," Eden said as she strode over to them.

"What now?"

"Scott is missing, too. So, now we have Marv missing and the boss we don't trust missing also."

"Do you think that Marv might have put his foot down and refused to help him?" Kap asked.

"Not sure if he would," El said.

"He might have. I got on the phone with Mom."

"I thought we weren't telling them anything," El said, irritation rolling through his voice.

"First, I didn't tell Mom, but she knows something's up. You know how she is."

"And she knows about Marv?"

She nodded. "Marv got passed over for a promotion. He was supposed to be moved up to a position that would oversee operations in the Asian theater."

El whistled, and Kap put the pieces together.

"You think that Scott passing him over was the straw that broke the camel's back?" he asked.

"Might be. Mom agrees. Marv found out about being passed over late yesterday. The fact that he disappeared off the face of the earth is probably not a good thing."

"He might have been in contact with people who would

investigate Scott. We both know that Marv has a real petty streak," El said.

Her phone buzzed and she looked down. "Sam said that there were a few texts sent out to a staffer for the Senate Intelligence Committee from Marv's phone."

"Fuck, that asshole," El said.

"What's going on?" Seth asked.

They gave him a rundown on everything that happened.

"Dammit. Sam said they found blood...a lot of it in Marv's car." Her face was pale, worry darkening her eyes. "I had my issues with Marv, but I need him to be okay."

She was right. She had good reason to never talk to Marv again after what happened three years ago, but he was like family, so he understood.

Her phone went off again, and she looked down at it.

"Eden?" Kap asked.

She drew in a deep breath and looked up. For a few moments, she looked lost, as if everything in her life was about to be ruined. Then, he saw her straighten to her full height. "Just more details on the car. None of it looks good."

He nodded.

"I need a sec."

"Are you okay?"

She smiled. "I'm fine. Just need to splash some water on my face and clear my mind."

"Sure thing."

He watched her head off down the hall that led to the bathrooms, then he rejoined the discussion.

"There isn't much we can do from here. First, it didn't happen here in Hawai'i," Del said.

"Our other problem is that we don't even know if this has anything to do with our investigation," Adam commented.

As they went round and round about what this meant for the investigation—which he knew in the end would lead to nothing at the moment—Kap's gut started to churn. Something was wrong, but he couldn't put his finger on it. He glanced at the clock and realized it had been close to fifteen minutes since Eden had walked off.

He frowned and started off in the direction of the bathrooms. Even without turning around, he knew that El was following him.

"What's up?"

"Your sister has been gone for a while."

El grunted but said nothing else as he followed him. He knew he couldn't just barge into the women's bathroom, so he knocked. The door opened to reveal Nikki.

"Is Eden in there?"

"No. It was empty when I came in."

Fuck. He whipped around and pulled up their security cameras. They all had access to them. Flicking through the history, he found the door that would allow Eden to slip away unnoticed. She even glanced up at the camera, her eyes sad, her expression telling him she was sorry. Of course, she knew that he would see it.

"Get hold of Sam," he told El as they hurried back into the common room. "Ask her to find your sister."

He was on the phone, already waiting for an answer.

"What's wrong?" Seth asked. Everyone turned around.

"Eden's missing." Panic threatened to choke Kap. He beat it back, barely, but he knew he had to keep his head screwed on straight. Eden needed him. She needed all of them.

"What do you mean her phone is on?" El shouted into the phone. And while Kap could understand that he was freaking out--they needed Sam's help.

He snatched El's phone out of his hand.

"What the fuck, Hanson?"

He ignored Eden's brother. Now was not the time to deal with his freak-out. Not when Kap was freaking out enough for the two of them.

"Sam, it's Kap."

"Well, thank goodness. El is losing it. Okay, her phone is on and she's walking. She didn't take a car."

"Of course. She doesn't have a car."

"*Please*. Dammit. Her phone just turned off, and I have a feeling she didn't do it."

"I'm going to put you on speaker."

"Okay."

He clicked on the speaker phone. The only sound they all heard was the keys tapping.

"Do you need anything from our end?" Seth asked.

"Maybe get into her cloud. I assume Dillon and Warner are still in the office?"

The two men in question looked at each other, then back at Kap. Dillon nodded.

"Yes."

"Have them tap into her cloud. She didn't have the contact phone on her person. I think she left that at her house when she bugged out. I'm tapping into the traffic cam history, so I can track her movements."

Dillon pulled out his phone and stepped away. Every little bit of surveillance they did sent Kap's panic higher. Sweat trickled down his back, and it wasn't even hot in the office.

More clicking.

"*Sam*," El said.

"I know. I'm hurrying." The tension in the office ratcheted up a notch every second that went by.

"Thanks, Em," Dillon said as he came back to the group. "Send it to my phone."

Then he hung up. The only person she texted with was Ian, according to Emily."

His phone buzzed, and his eyes narrowed. "Dammit, they used Ian."

He showed Warner, then he turned the phone so the rest of the room could see it. It was Ian, and he looked like he'd been worked over. His lip was split, and blood trickled out of his nose. His eyes were closed, and his hands were zip-tied.

"Shit," Autumn muttered. "I'm going to kill whoever put their hands on my brother."

"What is happening?" Sam said, all the while he heard her working on the keyboard.

"It's Ian. He's been taken."

Silence reigned. She wasn't even tapping on the keyboard.

"Sam?" Kap asked.

"Was it at his apartment?"

Autumn stepped closer to study the picture. "Yeah, that's his apartment."

"She was headed in that direction when her phone turned off." She started working again, from the sound of it. "Ian is like one of us, El."

Kap looked up at El.

"I didn't think about that. I was thinking US agents."

"What?"

"The idea that it was people with familial connections

who were targeted. Ian's father was MI-6. Sam, we need to see if Ian has a contract on his head."

Damn, they hadn't even thought of that. And someone had used her connection with Ian to lure her out. Of course, she went. Eden would never leave a partner behind to deal with a monster.

"He has several, or did, but most of them expired." She hadn't looked that up. She had already known. "You know agents are always in danger of that, especially someone like Ian."

"Let's go," Kap said, handing El the phone and striding out of the office. Eden's brother was hot on his heels.

"We need a plan," Seth said.

"We save Eden and Ian and arrest the bad guy if he's still alive."

"Hanson," Seth said, grabbing him by the arm. "You need to keep your head cool. Don't go in with your guns blazing."

As much as he would want to do that, he wouldn't put Eden at risk. He nodded, and Seth let go.

"Sirens off when we get close, folks," Seth said, as both teams of TFH strode out of the office. Eden and Ian were considered family in a way, and one thing TFH understood was taking care of their Ohana.

twelve

EDEN WALKED down the hallway to Ian's apartment. The area was quiet as most of the people in the condo were probably at work. She knew there was only one other person who lived on this floor because Ian liked his privacy.

As she neared the door, it struck her how odd it was that this had happened during the day, but, then again, it made sense in a way. She was at a safe house at night. There would be no way to get her away from there without her protection detail. If this were David Scott, it made a lot of sense. He had been a talented spy, according to her mother and father. He would make sure that no detail was overlooked.

At this moment, she wasn't even sure Ian was still alive. Eden knew it was a little reckless not to get proof of life, but she couldn't have done that without looking suspicious. She had made sure to look into the camera when she left. She'd left her phone on for as long as he had let her. The oversight was intentional, but Eden didn't know what it was about. More mind games. David Scott had always been a man who thrived on them.

She just hoped that she would be able to deal with what-ever happened and that she could hold off the kidnapper until Kap and TFH arrived.

Her fear climbed with each step, leaving her almost breathless. She couldn't give in to that because she knew what she had to do. Maybe it would be like when El had been taken. Then, the kidnappers had been inept. She knew she had surprised them thanks to Sam's help.

She hesitated at the door, regret holding her still for a moment. Why hadn't she told Kap she loved him? She knew with every fiber of her being that she would probably love him until the day she died. He might never find out if she fucked this up.

Pushing those thoughts aside, she tried the doorknob and wasn't surprised when it turned easily. With a deep breath, Eden opened the door and stepped inside Ian's apartment.

As they neared the apartment building, the sirens went silent. Kap's gut was tight with anxiety. He had done more than his fair share of rescues from kidnappers. He had worked with a K&R firm after leaving NCIS. This was different. Eden's life was at stake, and Kap wasn't ready for her to die. He couldn't lose her when he had just gotten her back. And definitely not before he could tell her he loved her.

He pulled up to the building, the tires of his SUV and the other TFH SUVs screeching. All of them slipped out of the vehicles, their battle mentality in place. Seth walked up to him.

"Your head still in the game?"

He nodded as he turned to El. "You've been here before?"

"Yeah. Ian's on the top floor, of course."

Yeah, of course. He could just imagine how much that would have gone for, but it wasn't the best choice for security. Being at the top of the condo building also meant that you would have fewer escape routes.

But it also meant they had a way to trap the bastard, causing so much pain.

"Sam, we're here. We're going up."

He hung up the phone and slipped it into his pocket. "Let's go get my sister."

Kap nodded, and they headed into the building. He would do everything he could to save her or die trying. There was no other alternative.

Eden had her gun out, ready to shoot, but she knew she had to be careful. With her back against the wall, she made her way into the living room. No one. It was weirdly quiet. It was as if all the air had been sucked out of the room. She took a second to draw in a deep breath before continuing on.

Making her way to the hallway that led to Ian's bedroom, she felt something shiver over her neck. Someone was watching, but she wasn't sure from where. Also, this seemed almost too easy. Walking right into the apartment, finding it so still and with no sign of violence left her off kilter.

Straitening her spine, she continued on. She found Ian in his bedroom, on the floor, leaning against the wall closest to her. His eyes were closed, and his hands were zip-tied. He looked even worse in person. A black eye, a broken nose, and a split lip were the first things she saw. She glanced around the room, still unsure of what was going on and who was there. She didn't know what she was going to find, but this quiet was ramping up her nerves.

She hadn't been an actual agent three years ago, but with the training she had, plus what Dillon had taught her, she now knew she could handle herself better. Still, it didn't make her feel any better that she felt glued to the floor for just a few seconds. The smart thing was to assess the situation, and, at the moment, it didn't look like anyone was there. Eden knew better.

Knowing that she was about to make herself a target, but not able to hold back any longer, she hurried to get to Ian. She huddled down close to him and felt for a pulse. Relief filled her as she felt a strong beat.

"I told you I wouldn't kill him."

She knew that voice. It stopped her in her tracks and stole her breath. She had heard it most of her life. Slowly, she turned around and found the man she had considered her uncle pointing a gun at her.

Shock should have been racing through her, but for some reason, it was resignation. Had she always suspected him, in the back of her mind? Maybe her subconscious had. This was the man who had spent holidays with them. He had been at her dance recital when she was twelve.

He was also the man who told her he couldn't help her find El.

Her fingers almost spasmed with the need to shoot him, but he shook his head. His stupid, bald head.

"I'll shoot him." There was no mistaking the deadly promise in those words. He didn't sound mad, just normal, which heightened her anxiety.

She held onto her gun for a second, then set it down.

Standing, she took him in. He looked like he always had. Custom suit, balding head, those glasses that never seemed to stay in place. His blue gaze studied her as if she were a bug.

"Why?"

He rolled his eyes; his whole expression reeked of irritation. "Why? That's such a boring discussion."

It took everything in her power not to scream at him. She just hoped that Kap and TFH had picked up on her location, or at least where she had been headed. Holding out until they showed up was key.

But she knew this man. Maybe not as well as she thought she had, but she did know his need for recognition. Trying her best to act nonchalant, she crossed her arms across her chest.

"Okay, don't tell me why you're a traitor. Doesn't really matter in the end."

His eyes narrowed. "What do you mean by that?"

"You could kill me and Ian, but everyone will know."

He snorted. "Doesn't matter with the amount of money I have. I'm disappearing after this."

"Oh, are you? Interesting. I mean, I get that you would want to hide since you're a traitor."

"I am not a traitor!"

"You killed agents. You *are* a traitor." Yeah, she was poking the bear, but she wanted him mad and distracted. If he were a true sociopath, she knew that it would take a lot to rock his foundation, at least at the moment. Many of them preferred to be in control of the situation.

"You always did have your mother's mouth on you. Maybe if she had learned to control it, I would have married her."

She threw her head back and laughed. Nothing was amusing in this conversation, but she needed to keep him engaged. The idea that her mother would *ever* have married this asshole was actually funny. From what her parents had told her, it was her mother who had proposed, not her father.

"Shut up," he said.

Eden stopped laughing, but she didn't hide her amusement. "You think my mother would have anything to do with you? Not when she could have a man like my father."

"She wanted his money. I didn't have anything other than my regular pay. Your mother is a gold digger."

"Funny that their marriage has lasted over thirty years."

He blinked.

"Oh, you didn't think about that, did you? Is that why you were killing agents? Because a woman hurt your little man feelings?"

"Shut it." Spittle flew from his mouth. He was solely concentrating on her now, and that's the way she wanted it. "I didn't just kill for the fun of it."

"No?"

"No." His lips curved up into a smile that chilled her blood. "I got fucking rich doing it."

The hits. He had sold out his fellow agents for the money. But there was something else in his voice. His need for power was dripping from every word, and she was betting on that to help her distract him until TFH could get here. Still, she read the implication in his eyes that now looked crazed. Was he really crazy, or was she imagining it?

"I get that. You're a traitor and a whore for money."

He moved closer to the window, closer to her and Ian. It also made it harder for him to see down the hallway.

"I guess it takes one to know one."

She would have laughed at his idiotic taunt. Instead, she cocked her head as she studied him. "How so?"

"That NCIS agent, Hanson. You were crazy about him."

"Oh, so you being paid to kill your fellow agents because some girl rejected you years ago is the same as a consensual relationship? You really have lost your mind."

"He never told you he was an asset?"

They had managed to get inside the apartment with the help of the management. He heard someone talking in what he assumed was the bedroom. El was behind him, along with the rest of TFH. Somewhere, standing guard in the hallway outside and in the stairwell. They had all their bases covered.

He got close enough to hear a man talking.

"He never told you he was an asset?"

He was talking about Kap. He wasn't sure how Marvin knew, but he could tell by the tone in his voice that he did. El tapped him on the shoulder. He glanced back, and El was holding up his phone. He had typed out Uncle Marv on a note app.

Kap nodded in acknowledgement.

"More lies," Eden said, her voice strong. "I'm wondering now if you can even tell the truth."

He fucking loved that woman. He knew she wasn't stupid, so she had to be worried about what Marv was going to do to her. But she didn't show it. Even though Kap couldn't see her, he knew she was standing with her spine straight and her gaze direct.

"How do you think he got approval so fast?"

Approval? He would have to ask about that later.

"He was an NCIS agent with top security clearance and a proven track record." There was a beat of silence. "I'm assuming you started to kill for the money, but we weren't the only ones who had hits taken out on us. I'm also assuming it was our connection to the CIA. Being legacies?"

"Always getting ahead without much work." Marv spat out the words, violence dripping from every syllable. This man had a grudge and a chip on his shoulder the size of the Diamond Head crater.

"There was one thing different about El and me. We were more assets, not agents. So our attempted murder was personal."

Again, silence filled the room.

"Oh, come on, *Uncle* Marv. You wanted any reminder of our mother's rejection to be extinguished."

"Like I said, you always did have a nasty mouth."

She might not have heard it, but what Kap heard in the other man's voice chilled his blood. He inched closer, keeping his chest tight against the wall. It would be the easiest way to see what was going on in that room. He couldn't look behind him, hoping that El kept his calm.

"Well, Marv, I say this with all due respect, fuck off."

Kap got a look at the other man's face. It was mottled with rage, his hand fairly shaking with it. He knew from the look in his eyes that he was going to shoot Eden. Fear shot through him as he rushed forward in the direction of her voice. He tackled her just as the gun went off. He felt a white-hot sting hit him on his side just as they fell to the floor.

"No!" Marv screamed as he pointed the gun at both him and Eden. She was pushing against him, trying to get him off of her, but he refused to budge.

"Drop it, Marv," El ordered.

"Fucking Carlyles," Marv said. But before he could shoot again, two shots rang out.

He heard someone fall to the ground. Kap lifted his head and found Ian holding a gun, even with his hands still zip-tied, and El keeping his weapon trained on Marv as he moved forward. He kicked the gun away from their old boss, even though Kap knew the man was dead. There were two shots in his chest. No one could survive that or the blood loss he was going through.

"Let me up, Kap."

He rolled off her, so she could see what was going on. When he rose, he felt another sting. Fucker got him with that shot, hitting his side. It didn't feel too bad.

"Is everyone all right?"

That was Adam striding into the room. Their earpieces were buzzing with a demand for answers.

"Yeah," he said as nausea rose up.

He heard everyone start talking at once, but he couldn't concentrate on anything. There was more buzzing, and it had nothing to do with his earpiece. Instead, he felt as if his head was swimming and the entire room was spinning. El and Eden helped Ian up, then she turned back to him.

He smiled...or he thought he did.

"Kap?" Worry filled her voice as her eyes widened with alarm. She rushed forward as he felt his knees give way.

Stumbling, he fell toward her. She caught him and tried to keep him upright.

"El, I need help."

"Shit," El said, running over. The twins laid Kap down, and that's when he felt the dampness on his back.

Why was he so weak? Why was the world seemingly going dark?"

"Kapone, do not do this! Do you hear me?"

He lifted his hand to her face. She was the most beautiful woman in the world to him. Always would be. Like now, when she was crying and a blubbering mess, she should look horrible, but she was still stunning.

He opened his mouth to say something, to tell her she was beautiful, but he couldn't seem to talk.

"There is so much blood. Why is there blood?" Hysteria edged her voice up another octave.

"Hey, everything is okay, babe," he said, finally able to speak.

"Stop talking. Save your strength. Get the fucking EMTs up here now!"

He smiled. "I love you."

Her eyes widened, and a fresh set of tears filled them. "Don't say things like that in that voice. You will be okay."

He felt his smile fade as the entire world around him went dark.

thirteen

"NO!" Eden screamed the word, her entire world dissolving as she watched Kap's eyes close. "Don't you die on me, Kapone. Do you hear me?"

She was pulling off his damned bulletproof vest, her brother taking over the job when her hands started to shake too much. When he finally got it off, she noticed that blood soaked one side of his shirt. It had been the side that faced Marv when he'd fired.

Fighting back tears and nausea, she lifted his shirt and saw the bullet hole. Terror seemed to grip her lungs, and she had to force the air through them. This couldn't be happening. She could not lose him because of something she did.

"You are not allowed to do this. Do you fucking understand me, Kapone? Don't you leave me."

There was so much blood. He shouldn't be hurt. The vest should have protected him, but he had tackled her to save her life. She had been the cause of this, and she would never forgive herself for it.

He couldn't die on her. If he did, Eden didn't know if

she would be able to go on. Fear iced her heart as she tried to stop the blood, but there was just so much of it. It gushed up through her fingers.

"EMTs are here, Eden," El said as he dragged her away. "You need to stay out of their way."

She knew that, and she complied, but every second that ticked by felt like hours. Years. El held her tight as the EMT looked Kapone over before putting him on the stretcher. As they wheeled him away, she wrenched herself away from her brother and ran after them. They were going to take her in that ambulance. There was no way she would wait around to be taken there.

Her brother was hot on her heels as they got onto the elevator with Kap and the EMTs.

"There's not enough room in the ambulance for everyone," one of them said. She looked at the man, then at her brother.

"I'm going with you."

There was no way Eden would let him go to the hospital by himself. She would be there with him the entire way.

"I'll get someone to take me," El said.

She nodded. Her brother helped her into the ambulance because her knees were too weak. She moved to the back out of the way, but she wanted to hold his hand. Eden knew she would be in the way if she did that, so she settled in the corner and watched the EMT work. Her gaze focused on Kap. His skin was usually dark, but it was ashen now from the loss of blood.

"Ma'am, are you okay?"

She glanced at the EMT and realized he was talking to her. Of course he was. It was just Kap, Eden, and the EMT.

It seemed to take a lot of effort, but she nodded. "It's Kap's blood. He saved me."

"That's the officer's name?"

She nodded. "Kap Hanson."

"Are you his next of kin?"

She shook her head. "No. His family is back in Georgia."

God, his mother would never forgive her if anything happened to Kap. She had never met the woman, but she knew she was a strong influence in his life, and he loved her. It was one of the things that drew her to him. A man who could admit he loved his mom and showed it was a treasure.

She bit her lip to keep it from trembling. The sirens were blasting, but she didn't seem to hear them. All she focused on was Kap and his chest. If it kept moving, everything would be okay. She kept repeating that to herself the entire ride.

They rushed to Tripler Army Medical Center, and she jumped out the minute the doors opened. She wanted to make sure she stayed out of their way. There was a team waiting, as if they had been alerted to a trauma case.

She watched as they wheeled him into the hospital, and she felt her head start to spin. She could not lose him. They had already lost years away from each other, and he'd said he loved her. She wanted to say it back, to see him flash that amazing smile at her.

"Ma'am," a woman said. Eden blinked and looked at her. She was a younger woman wearing scrubs. "Are you okay?"

Eden nodded. "This is Kap's blood."

Understanding lit her eyes, and sympathy moved over her expression. "You want to come inside? We can get you washed up while they work on Kap."

"Eden!"

Without turning around, she knew that was her brother.

"That's my brother."

The woman nodded. "You all should come inside, and we can get you some scrubs."

"Thank you," El said, slipping his arm around her. He pulled her closer to him, wrapping his arms completely around her. Even in the sun, she felt cold, as if it were the middle of winter in Montana.

"He's gonna be okay, Ed."

She leaned back and looked up at him. "Don't lie to me. We don't do that, not when it comes to the important stuff. You saw all the blood. He passed out, and he said he loved me. I didn't get a chance to tell him."

"Tell him what?" he asked softly.

"I love him. I love him so fucking much, and I didn't get to tell him," she said, not caring how loud she was or what a mess she was. "I've loved him for years, and I wasted time. He got hurt trying to save me. It was my fault."

"Stop that. It is not your fault. It was Marv's fault. He shot him. He's the bastard who caused us so much pain. Do not blame yourself!"

She couldn't fight it now. The welling panic took over, and she collapsed in his arms, sobbing because the one man she would always love was fighting for his life, and he didn't even know that she loved him. She knew it was self-centered to be worried about this when his life hung in the balance. When he woke up, she would tell him, and she would prove it every day of their lives.

Kap felt as though he was floating in a sea of white clouds. He knew he had to be on some major drugs...or was he dead. No. He couldn't be dead. He refused to allow his declaration of love to Eden to go unanswered. Because when he felt that bullet hit him, he had only one thought—and that was how much he loved Eden. There would never be another woman like her in his life, and he would not accept that he had lost his chance.

He moved, and even as he floated on a drug-coated dream, pain filtered through him.

"Fuck."

"Well. That's not a very nice thing to say."

That was not Eden. That was El, and Kap frowned. He thought he might have frowned. He wasn't really sure if he had or not.

With great effort, he forced his eyes to open. Bright light hit his eyes, and he slammed them shut again.

"Fuck."

"Is that the only word you know? This could get really embarrassing when you have to answer questions for the CIA."

Smart ass. "Turn the light down."

"Oh, sorry." He heard El move. "Okay."

This time, when he opened his eyes, there was only a soft light on in the room. He sighed in relief.

"Are you with us?"

"What?"

"You woke up a few times, but you weren't really with us."

"Where's Eden?"

"She's across the hall talking to the CIA. She refused to leave the hospital. Please talk to her about that. She's looking rough."

He tried to swallow, but his mouth and throat were dry. "How long?"

El walked over to a table that had some cups and water on it. He brought Kap some water. El held it as Kap took a long sip out of the straw.

"Thanks," he said, now even more exhausted.

"No problem. I was put on Kap duty."

"How long?"

"You've been out of surgery for about thirty-six hours. It was a near thing." He sighed. "I'm glad you survived."

"That's two of us."

He shook his head. "Not sure you remember what happened when it all went down, but my sister... let's just say she wouldn't have been okay."

The door opened. "Kap."

He turned in the direction of the sweetest sound he had ever heard. She rushed to his side.

"Hey, babe."

Tears filled her eyes.

"Don't cry."

She shook her head. "I've been so worried. The doctors said you were fine, and it was normal that you weren't coherent for a few days, but I didn't like it."

He tried to reach out to take her hand, but he was already feeling exhausted. She took his hand and leaned down to kiss him. He could taste the salt of her tears before she pulled back.

"Well, that was gross."

She shook her head and looked at her brother. "Thank you for watching him. Mom and Dad should be here soon. Do you mind meeting them downstairs?"

"Gladly, this was a disgusting display."

But Kap heard the humor in her brother's voice.

"Glad you're not dead," he said before he left the room, leaving them alone. Finally.

"Are you okay?" he asked.

She smiled. "Yes. Thanks to you."

Then her smile faded.

"What?"

"I'm sorry I lied to you before. Marv had threatened Ian if I told anyone. I tried my best to leave clues."

Relief hit him. "Don't. Sam got them easily. I'm not mad at you."

She sighed and leaned against his bed.

"I have something I need to say to you, though."

"What?"

The door opened as he opened his mouth. A doctor came in—or at least he assumed it was a doctor.

"Oh, I see we're awake," the older man said. He appeared to be in his fifties. From the haircut and the way he held himself, Kap realized he was at Tripler.

"I know I badgered you," Eden said. "I'm sorry."

The doctor's expression softened. "No worries." Then he looked at Kap again. "I'm Dr. Adams, one of the surgeons who fixed you up. If Eden will give us a moment?"

He knew she didn't want to go, but she nodded. "I'll be right outside,"

"That woman loves you," Dr. Adams said. "Hope you don't mind me telling you that. She came in with you and hasn't left. We've tried to get her to go rest, but she's refused."

"That's because she's the most amazing woman in the world."

Eden was still jittery as she walked up and down the hallway. She knew he was fine, and he actually looked ten times better than he had in the middle of the night. Color had come back into his face, and she was happy to say that he seemed to have made it out of the woods. Still, she wouldn't get over the sight of him like that any time soon.

She noticed that a woman went into Ian's room. Security was tight at Tripler, so she figured it was another CIA agent wanting to talk to Ian. She had been dressed like one in a suit and heels. Before Eden could think about that too much, the door to Kap's room opened.

"Your Kapone is a strong man. I think he is going to be just fine."

Drawing in a deep breath, she let the doctor's comments filter through her worry. She knew Kap looked better, but hearing it from Dr. Adams was more reassuring than just seeing the evidence before her. From the moment he walked up and told her, Kap would have a long recovery ahead of him. He needed rest because of the blood loss. The fact that Marv had hit the one place on his upper body, other than his head, that the vest didn't protect was one of the weirdest things to ever happen.

He would have been fine, but the bullet had nicked an artery, and if TFH hadn't called an ambulance to be on standby, Kap would probably be dead.

"Thank you for everything."

He nodded and headed off down the hallway. Drawing in a deep breath, she stepped back into the room. The moment Kap saw her, he broke into a smile.

"Come here," he said.

She did, but she took her time. Now that she was ready to tell him she loved him, she was scared. What if he hadn't really meant it? A lot of people said things they didn't mean when they thought they were dying.

"Can you take that thing down?" he asked, tapping the bed guards. She nodded and did as he asked. He patted the mattress. "Come here."

When he said the words this time, his voice was deeper. His Georgia accent rolled through her, blasting her with heat. She did as he asked. He took her hand, but she found it hard to make eye contact.

"What's wrong?"

"Nothing." God, she sounded like an idiot. For the last two days, she had wanted to tell him she loved him, but now she was being a coward.

"Everything after I got shot is hazy."

"Yeah?"

"I think I told you I loved you."

She nodded.

"I don't remember you telling me the same. Is that why you're acting weird? You are about to break things off?"

She made eye contact with him. "No. I..." she sighed, courage fading.

"Babe, tell me."

"I love you."

He didn't react right away, and she worried that he regretted his declaration. Then, his lips curved, and soon he was giving her that fantastic smile of his. It was brighter than the sun.

"Good, because I love you."

Happiness burst through her, and she smiled at him. "That's good."

He patted his shoulder. "You look tired. Beautiful, but tired. Why don't we take a little nap?"

Now that Eden knew he was safe and that she loved him, the last couple of days hit her. "That sounds like a great idea."

The woman known as Sam stood near the door, unable to proceed further into the room. She didn't like hospitals. They reminded her too much of the night her parents had died.

She pushed that thought out of her head. That wasn't important right now. Now, she had to ensure that Ian was truly safe. She had waited almost two days before she came, but she had to make sure things had calmed down. As it was, she'd practically run into David Scott. He looked a little worse for wear, but the man still made the trip over to Hawai'i. She would give him that.

"Are you going to stand there gawking at me?"

She hesitated, then walked closer. She had done a lot to

make herself unassuming. Walking through the halls of a military facility had her nerves stretched tight. The suit might be the reason. She hated to dress like this, but she knew how the CIA worked.

When she saw him, she fought the gasp. Ian was a handsome man with movie-star looks. Right now, he looked like he'd had the shit beat out of him. He had a black eye and a broken nose, even though it looked like it was healing fine.

"There you are. So, you decided to come in person to mock me."

She frowned. "No. I wanted to check in on you. Everyone said you were okay, but I wanted to make sure. Why would I mock you?"

He frowned, and, of course, he looked even sexier doing so. How could a man look so sexy all beat up? This was what was wrong with the world.

"Bellows got the drop on me."

She cocked her head. There, in his voice, she heard the recrimination. She straightened and looked him straight in the eye. Those beautiful blue eyes.

Stop thinking things like that.

"Bellows killed at least nine agents, maybe more. I think it's no big deal that he got the drop on you. Surviving is the important part."

His eyes narrowed. "Indeed."

Dammit, when he got all perturbed and talked like that, his disdain was easy to hear, it got her hot. Mainly because there had to be something wrong with her.

"I have to go."

"But you just got here." Sarcasm dripped from his words.

"I just wanted to make sure you're okay."

He opened his mouth, but she shook her head and started backing up. The door opened behind her, and she twisted around, ready to defend Ian. A nurse smiled at her.

"Hello. I'm here to take Mr. Smith's vitals."

She was young and smiling, as if she had won some kind of prize. Taking Ian's vitals was a prize most women would be willing to fight over.

"Make sure you take care of yourself," she said, hurrying to the door, needing to get out, to be free of this building.

"Sam," he called out, but she ignored him.

Hurrying to the stairwell, she started her long descent to the first floor. She slipped on a pair of sunglasses, hiding her eyes. Having two different colored eyes tended to attract attention. She hadn't had time to put her contacts in. With more bravery than she actually had, she strode through the first floor, nodding to a few people she recognized from the CIA. None of them recognized her. Why would they? She didn't look anything like she had back when she worked with them.

As she stepped out into the sun, she drew in a deep breath of the perfumed air and started to her car. She needed to get out of there before anyone recognized her.

Eden's head was on his chest, and his arm was wrapped around her. Having her by his side made everything right in his world. He wasn't sure exactly how this would look, but he wanted to be by her side.

They had time to figure it out. There was a clatter in the hallway, and her head popped up.

"Damn, that's my parents."

"What?"

"I know it isn't ideal. I mean, we just got back together, and we have to see if we can make this work—"

"There is no seeing. We *will* make this work."

She gave him a small smile. "Well, either way, that's our parents, I think. Even for former CIA assets, they can be kind of...well...Texan."

"No problem."

Then he heard an unmistakable voice.

"Where is my boy?"

His gaze collided with Eden's.

"Surprise?"

"How did you get them here so fast?"

"Mom and Dad took the jet."

El and Eden lived so modestly that Kap sometimes forgot that they were the children of billionaires.

"Don't be mad."

"Not mad." He smiled and shook his head. "Thank you."

She smiled. "I love you, Kapone Hanson."

"Remember that once you meet my mama."

She was laughing when she kissed him.

epilogue

KAP BROUGHT the last box of his belongings into Eden's house.

No. *Their* house. They were going to build a life here together. It was fast, he knew that, but once you realized you loved a person and that you would always love that person, you wanted to start your life right away. Also, near-death experiences tend to make you look at things differently.

"What a self-satisfied look," Ian said from the kitchen, sarcasm dripping from his voice.

He smiled at Eden's partner. While Kap didn't go back to work for another ten days, Ian had taken less than a week off. TFH had kept them all updated on the tangled web of murders linked to Marv. Other than taking the hits, Marv seemed to be working alone. He used people to help him, but the killing, well, he liked doing that himself.

"Do I look smug?"

"You do."

"Well, there's a reason."

Ian crossed his arms over his chest. "And what would that be?"

"I'm starting my life with the love of my life."

Ian rolled his eyes, but even when he did, Kap got the feeling that he was happy for them.

"I hear you're going to Vegas," he said, setting the box down on the coffee table.

"Yeah. Family trip, which should be interesting since that has never been something this family has done before."

"So your father and Adam's mom aren't eloping?"

Ian's eyes widened, startled. "No. What makes you ask that?"

No reason other than to screw with him. The entire TFH team still got a kick out of the former spy master romancing Adam Lee's mom.

He shrugged. "I do know your sister has some kind of other plan."

"My sister always has another plan. Seth doesn't know what kinds of headaches she is going to give him."

"I have a feeling my captain knows about the headaches and doesn't care." No, he loved the crazy woman. "So, you aren't meeting up with someone in particular?"

Everyone at TFH knew that Ian's nemesis had visited him in the hospital.

"No."

"No? I thought maybe Sam would be there."

His eyes narrowed as he studied Kap.

"Stop the gossiping and get the rest of the boxes," Eden called down. He smiled. She had been lighter these last few weeks, much like those days when they had first met.

"All the boxes have been brought in."

"Oh, good." She started down the steps, a smile curving her lips, and he couldn't help the burst of heat that sped through his blood. He would never forget just how it felt to have this woman look at him this way.

"Ugh, stop looking at her like that," Ian said.

"I concur," El said as he strode into the house.

"I thought you weren't coming home until tomorrow?" Eden asked.

"Job ended early."

"Do we want to know what that means?" Ian asked.

"Nope. And whatever Emily says to you is a lie."

"Well, I must make haste, as they say in my home country."

"That's not something they say. Is it?" El asked. "I mean, I know they did at one time, but...where have I heard that before?"

"Bridgerton," Eden said. "And don't even deny you watch it."

El said nothing.

"I was thinking we could all go out for dinner tonight," El said.

"Well..." Eden said.

They had planned on their own celebration, thinking that El wouldn't be back for a day or two.

"They have plans," Ian said, grabbing El by the arm. "Come tell me all the bad things Emily did to you while you were on assignment, and we can plot her demise."

After the door shut behind them, Eden came to him, slipping her arms around his waist. "Finally."

He chuckled. "Ian helped us with the last of the boxes."

TFH had helped him move the furniture he didn't sell, but that was over the weekend. Today was Tuesday, and while he could have waited until the weekend, he had wanted to get moved in as quickly as possible. Plus, he would go back to work next week—light duty.

"Whatever will we do?" he said.

"I thought we could start unpacking."

He looked down at her and saw the teasing smile on her face. "Hmm, well, we are close to the kitchen."

They'd christened many of the rooms and spaces in the house, but the kitchen hadn't made the cut.

"True, but we have a lot of boxes to unpack."

The sweet teasing in her voice made his heart soar.

"Naw," he said, bending down and picking her up in his arms. She always felt right when he did this, like a puzzle piece he had been missing for a long time. He could be irritated with the loss of time, but he wouldn't. Every experience had brought them to this ending...or beginning, really.

He set her on the counter. She was smiling at him, her joy surrounding him.

"You have on too many clothes," he said.

He grabbed the bottom of her shirt and pulled it over her head. She was laughing when he pulled her board shorts down her legs. He decided to spend the rest of his life making her happy.

Pulling her to the edge of the counter, he spread her thighs to step between them.

"I thought you were hungry," she said.

"I am, and I intend to feast on you." He said as he kissed his way down her body.

They could worry about food later, because, as he said, he had a feast to devour. He kissed each of her thighs before setting his mouth against her hot, wet pussy. The sweet taste of her danced over his tongue. His dick twitched with need, but he ignored it. Right now, it was all about Eden. She moaned his name, a sound he would never get sick of hearing. He teased her with his tongue, his lips, and his fingers. Soon, she was coming apart, screaming his name as she bucked up against his mouth.

When he rose to his feet, his hands were shaking. Kap was sure she would cause this reaction until the day he died.

He didn't undress. He couldn't. He just undid his pants. His cock was eager, ready to thrust into her.

"Eden."

She was laid out on the counter, her skin flushed, and a smile curving her lips. He centered the head of his dick at her core, entering her with one hard thrust. They both moaned, and he held himself still for a second. Eden wrapped her legs around him, and he started to move.

Her inner muscles clung to him, seemingly pulling him deeper into her warmth.

"Yes, god, yes, Kap!" She came again, bowing up like before, her hands on her nipples. It was one of the most erotic things he had ever witnessed. And it was his undoing. He drove into her once more, before pleasure exploded within and he poured himself into her.

They were both breathing heavily. She looked up at him, her heavy-lidded gaze sending another wave of need through him.

"I love you," he said.

She dropped her legs from around his waist, and she

raised up to kiss him. "I love you too. But, if you don't feed me, I'm not sure I'll have the strength to keep this up."

"You got it."

Then he stepped back, pulling out of her, buttoning himself up, and picking her up off the counter. "We do need to shower before we go out, right?"

"Of course," she said with a laugh as he carried her up the stairs. Yep, he was happy and damned smug, and he didn't give a damn who knew. All he cared about was that he and Eden were in this together.

Three days later.

His phone was buzzing much like he was. He snorted. BUZZZZ.

And this is why he didn't drink. The truth was, he was a real lightweight. It was one of the reasons he laughed at the jokes about him being 007. He hated martinis, shaken or stirred.

But after what his sister had just pulled off, drinking had been the only recourse.

He blinked, looking at the hallway. Was this his floor? All the hotel hallways looked the same. His phone started buzzing again, and since it could be work, he pulled it out. *Unknown number.*

Well, that could be only one person, and he wanted to avoid her. Granted, he hadn't heard from her in almost a month since he'd been in the hospital. Finally, it stopped buzzing, and, immediately, he hated that he'd been an ass and not answered. She would probably try his sister.

But no sooner than he thought that, his phone started to buzz again.

"What?"

"You need to get to your room."

He frowned. "How do you know where I am?"

"I'm going to assume that you're still drunk, or you would never ask me such an asinine thing. Get in your room. Now!"

Her voice had risen to a near shout, and he pulled the phone away from his ear. Then he put it back.

"No shouting. Besides, I'm not sure I'm on the right floor."

"You are. Get to your room now."

"And why do I have to do that?"

"Because there are two men on their way up to kill you. So, for the love of all that is holy, Ian, get your cute ass in your room!"

Thank you so much for reading Justified Lies! If you loved the book, please think about leaving a review at your favorite retailer or online review site.

If you want to find out why actually happens in Vegas, be sure to pick up Devious Delectable Decades Anthology which will include the never before seen short, Justified Escape. It's on preorder now and includes a lot of very talented authors.

Sam and Ian are finally getting their book in 2026! You can preorder Burned from your favorite retailer!

If you would like to see how TFH all started, you can grab SEDUCTIVE REASONING featuring Del and Emma for FREE at your favorite retailer.

seductive reasoning is free!

If you would like to see how TFH all started, you can grab SEDUCTIVE REASONING featuring Del and Emma for FREE at your favorite retailer.

He's got a killer to catch and no time for love. Fate has other plans.

Former Army Special Forces Officer **Martin "Del" Delano** has enough on his hands chasing a serial killer and heading up TASK FORCE HAWAII. He definitely doesn't need the distraction of **Emma Taylor**. From the moment they meet, she knocks him off his feet, literally. Unfortunately, she's the best person to have on the team to make the connections to help them catch their killer.

For Emma, it's hard to ignore the lure of a man like him. Tats, muscles and his Harley cause her to have more than a few fantasies about Del. He'd never be interested in a geek like her, but she can't resist toying with him. When she pushes the teasing too far, she ends up in his bed. She convinces herself she can handle it until the moment he steals her heart.

Del can't help falling for the quirky genius. She's smart,

funny and there's a sweet vulnerable side to her that only he can see. As Emma gets more involved with the investigation, she becomes the target of the psychopath. When the danger escalates, Del promises to do anything to save the woman who not only captured his heart but also his soul.

Martin Delano stepped out of his pickup and shut the door, as a light trade wind danced over his skin. He slipped his shoulder holster on, then looked up and down the street. Finding no traffic, he jogged over to the other side, following the lights set up by the Honolulu Police Department.

Being former military, he should be used to the early morning wakeup calls, but it didn't mean he had to be happy about it—especially this morning. The lights burned his eyes. Damn, he was getting old when he couldn't seem to make it up and at work without a cup of coffee. He should have grabbed one before he left his house in Hawaii Kai.

Police tape marked off the spot, and a very serious looking young officer in uniform stood by the entrance. His militant expression told Del this was his first big assignment. The kid raised his hand as if to stop him...or die trying. God save him.

He wasn't in the mood.

"HPD only, sir," he said, his voice stern.

Del sighed and pulled out his Task Force badge. He'd been there a year and people in the department still didn't know who he was. Of course, the officer looked like he was straight out of the academy, so that was probably the reason. However, the department was small, and Del had been on TV enough that he thought everyone knew his face. And, as the local members of his team kept telling him, everyone knows everyone else on the island.

The officer's face reddened. "Sorry, sir."

Del nodded and attached the badge back onto his belt. "I'm looking for Rome Carino."

"Of course, sir." He turned and motioned with his hand. "He's right over there, by the Medical Examiner."

Del glanced over and saw where he was talking about. There was a barrier set up along the opposite side of the bridge. That would have been done probably before the ME had shown up.

"Mahalo," Del said, as he walked past the officer towards the ME. He passed a few familiar faces. Some smiled, some frowned, and others barely acknowledged his existence.

The air was muggy from the recent rain, and the sun would start rising soon. Traffic in Honolulu was always a bitch. The influx of tourists added to the locals' aggravation, but figure in the water main breaks and the rail construction, it could be a real pain in the ass. Being Monday made it worse, and the McCully Bridge over the Ala Wai Canal was always busy.

As he approached the group, he noticed a handful of detectives he knew. He had been there for a year now, and he still felt like an outsider. Being a Haole didn't make for easy detective work in Hawaii. Not to mention, a few of them thought he shouldn't have been given the job. Carino had been offered the job at one time, but he declined. Now, Del was starting to understand why.

Del knew it was a bad sign when Carino called him. Del's team only handled the major crimes, the ones that would require more than a little diplomacy working with various law enforcements. Not that he was always good with diplomacy, but in other words, Carino didn't want the headache.

He noticed Drew Franklin, the ME assistant. Nice kid, local, tall and skinny, with a world class mind and an irritating habit of trying too hard. But he was good on the job, even if he did have an odd sense of humor, and an odd choice in clothing. He was wearing a pair of jeans today, his regular sneakers, and a T-shirt that said 'I like big books and I cannot lie.'

"Howzit, Del, I just got here too."

Del nodded. "Did you get the call?"

He pushed his horn-rimmed glasses back up the bridge of his nose. "Dr. Middleton called. She said I didn't need to be here, but I thought maybe Cat would be called out."

"Nope, I was on call last night, so I took the call."

"Makes sense."

"I'm glad you think so," he said, his voice dripping with sarcasm, but it went over Drew's head.

He just smiled as they walked together. The closer they got to the scene, Del's worry grew. He knew it was a dead woman, but for him to be called out, it had to be huge. Maybe a celebrity or dignitary. That meant it would hit the news services soon. Damn, he hated dealing with the press.

Carino noticed him and turned to greet him. Lean and tall, with feral eyes, he'd moved to Hawaii from Seattle several years earlier. The homicide detective had been one of the most welcoming in the HPD. His wife had insisted on inviting him over for dinner several times. A lot of folks weren't happy when they hired an outsider like him, but

Carino had been a transplant also, and Del had an idea he had wanted to make everyone know that he accepted him.

"Sorry about calling you out, Del, but Dr. Middleton thought it was important. Usually, I go with her gut, and when she showed me, I was sure of it."

He nodded. "No problem."

Carino looked at Drew. "Dr. Masterson could use some help."

"Of course," Drew said and hurried off, almost tripping over his larger than average feet in the process.

Carino and he watched Drew greet the doctor with as much enthusiasm as he had Del.

Del shook his head. Was he ever that young and eager? He couldn't remember, but he was sure that he had been when he entered the military. When he turned back to Del, he offered him a grim smile.

"Man, to be that young again," he said, voicing Del's thoughts.

Del nodded. "Makes me tired just listening to him sometimes."

Carino's smile faded. "I didn't want to say anything in front of him, not yet, but I have a bad feeling this might be a serial."

Del knew Carino wasn't jumping to conclusions. When there had been a serial killer terrorizing Honolulu, and especially the BDSM club members at Rough 'n Ready, he had been at the head of the case. He had caught the killer no one else had expected—with the help of an FBI agent, who had later become his wife. Carino did not make assumptions.

A heavy lead weight started to tighten in his stomach. This was going to be a fucking nightmare. He just knew it.

And, it would put his team to the test again. He didn't have a background in investigative work. Being an Army Ranger did give you a skill set that helped out in some things, but investigating a serial killer was different. Thank God he had a team with more experience in that department. Both Cat and Adam were in the department during Carino's investigation. And he knew his ME had experience with that kind of thing.

"What makes you think that? Does it resemble any other killings?"

The detective shook his head. "No, but she was posed, grotesquely. There's just something about the way she was left..." he sighed and rubbed his temples.

"Long night?"

Carino nodded. "Yeah, and I was just thinking I was getting too old for this."

"Nothing going on with Maria?"

He knew the detective's wife was pregnant and entering the final few months.

Flashing Del a smile, Carino shook his head. "No, just horrible insomnia for her, which means I have it because she wanders through the house constantly." His smile faded. "It's going to be a bitch of a day today, considering who I think is down there."

His head was already pounding from the lack of caffeine, and this was just ramping it up to a whole other level of pain.

"Who?"

Carino looked toward the scene, then back at Del. "We have to wait for official word, but I think it's Grace Singh."

The name hit him like a ton of bricks.

"Well, fuck."

Del knew the story. Hell, everyone in Hawaii knew the

story. Two weeks earlier, a pretty schoolteacher had disappeared. Right off the street in a good part of town.

There was no sign of her anywhere, which was definitely odd. From all accounts, she was sweet and unassuming, a bit of a homebody who lived with her parents—not an uncommon occurrence considering the housing situation on the island at the moment.

When the news had hit, everyone had shown up to help. Honolulu might be a big city to some, but Hawaii still operated like a small town. When one of their own went missing, especially a cherished teacher, they called out the reserves. Citizens, law enforcement, everyone. They all had looked for her and could not find one bit of evidence as to her whereabouts.

"Exactly. I wouldn't normally jump to conclusions, but she's fresh, and I know her face, of course. That means she has been alive the last two weeks. And, it's bad. There is no doubt in my mind someone tortured her."

Fuck. Nightmare did not cover it. They would get attention from the mainland on this one, and they always sent the local press into a frenzy.

"Okay."

They walked side-by-side down to the scene. With each step they took, he felt the weight of the oncoming investigation. This was going to be a bitch—and more than anything, he wanted to do right by the woman. Her poor family had been so sure they would find her alive, and now they would forever be without one part of the whole.

No one deserved to die like this.

"Hey, Elle, how's it going?" Del asked.

Dr. Elle Middleton was an English transplant, and one of

the best in her field. He knew he was damned lucky she had been assigned to his team when she had arrived in Hawaii.

"Hullo, Del. Not good, especially for this young woman."

She stood up and wiped her forehead with the back of her wrist. Since she'd cut her light blond hair, the fringe of it appeared just above her blue-green eyes. He read the horror in her gaze. This was not going to be pleasant for anyone.

"You got a time of death?"

"Within the last six hours from the liver temp. I would say less than three when she was actually found. She was left here after the rain stopped."

"Yeah?" Carino asked.

Elle nodded. "The impressions of shoes are there and there," she said pointing to the ground. "Drew is going to take a cast of them, but I am not sure we will find anything particularly important in that. They look pretty common. So, I'm assuming he waited on purpose until the rain was done. That ended about half past eleven last night here in Honolulu."

Del sighed and shook his head. "Poor woman."

"Indeed. I can tell you more when I get her on the table, but this woman went through hell."

"Show me what you have right now."

"Hey, I have a meeting with the brass at the top of the hour. They wanted an update. Call me if you need anything."

"Sure. Give my love to Maria," Del said as Carino slapped him on the shoulder and walked away.

He turned back around just as Elle moved and he finally saw the body. The memory of the smiling picture did not even seem like the same woman. Her eyes were closed, but he knew they were dark, always twinkling in all the photos. She was short in stature, five three if he remembered correctly, with short hair, and probably weighed no more than one hundred pounds. At least she had. If she had been posed, she had been moved, probably by Elle.

"We have pictures of her body before she was moved?"

"Yes," she said irritated.

He looked up and offered her a smile. "Sorry about that. Just thinking things through, and I didn't know who was here first. You know I am still new at all of this."

Elle sighed. "Sorry. Knowing just how bad it was...it hurts."

He heard the memory in her voice. "I understand." And he did. Elle would comprehend what Grace Singh had endured more than most others.

She straightened her shoulders, then squatted down. "If you look here, she was tied up."

She held up the hand of the woman and pointed to her wrist. He saw the burns on her wrists. Some light, some dark, and with different patterns pressed into her flesh.

It was done with some kind of rope, and probably impossible to narrow down.

"Her ankles are in the same condition."

"And the different shades of the bruising?"

"Repeated injuries. And with different ropes from the burns. So, he kept her like this for some time. Probably the entire time she was there. I'm pretty sure of sexual assault, but I will verify that in the lab. There are also burns on her body."

He squatted down beside her and looked over the body. There were small cylindrical burns over her flesh. Scabs had formed over some of them, while others were fresh.

Jesus.

"Looks like a cigarette lighter from a car."

"Yes. Bastard really hurt her. This isn't just about power. This is more about pain, and getting off on it. He should not be allowed in public."

Her voice wavered at the end, and he knew what it cost her.

"We'll get him, Elle."

She nodded, but said nothing else as he stood and looked over the crowd. It was early, but there was always some kind of hum in the early morning there—especially on a Monday. Hell, that's probably why the sick fuck had left her there on that particular day. More coverage, with a frenzy that would last for the entire week.

He saw one of the detectives taking pictures, and he wandered over to him.

"Did you get the crowd?"

"Yeah," he said. "But I was going to take a few more because it is really gaining attention."

He pulled out his card and gave it to him. "Could you make sure you get those to me as soon as possible?"

"With pleasure," he said, grim determination filling his voice.

Del paused, then the detective said, "I knew her. We went to the same school, a few years apart. A real sweetheart. Always had a smile for everyone."

Del nodded. That was the thing about Hawaii. Everyone had about six degrees of separation, or less. Either they knew Grace, or they knew someone who knew her. Her disappearance had been the focal point of the Hawaiian news shows since she had disappeared. And now, their focus would be on a killer.

The crowd was growing by the second, and he knew it would only be minutes before the news crews showed up. As if on queue, they appeared, screaming to a halt. He saw Jin Phillips, one very irritating newswoman, jump out of the van. Damn, the woman got on his nerves. She stood by, waiting for her crew before she attacked. And it would be an attack. The woman didn't know how to deal with news any other way.

Del looked away from her and up the canal toward Diamond Head. The scent of plumeria hit him, and he realized he was standing by a bush filled with them. It was usually something he liked to smell, but now, he knew he would always associate it with Grace Singh and her last night on earth.

The sun was just starting to peek over the crater. The brilliant streaks of orange and yellow lightened the sky. Even after a year, the beauty of it still stunned him. Del didn't think he would ever get used to the sight.

He looked back at the scene as Drew helped Elle put Grace Singh in a body bag, then lift her up onto the gurney. The buzz of the crowd was growing, and he could already hear Jin asking annoying questions.

Just another day in paradise.

returning in
december—>

THE BOSS

Loving her means it's more than his heart at risk.

Sick of the spy game, former CIA operative Vic Walker takes time off from his security firm to figure out just what he wants out of life. But peace and quiet isn't in the cards with a former business partner and ex-lover like MacKenzie Donovan.

Mac doesn't like asking for help from anyone, but this latest case has her in a little over her head. She crashes back into Vic's life with the CIA, the Russian Mob, and the FBI, on her tail after a job goes south.

But even as old feelings rise to the surface while they're busy dodging bullets, the authorities, and mobsters, they'll need to get out alive before they can have a second chance at love.

Author Note: This book includes two lovers who would

rather deal with murdering bad guys than with their feelings, a dysfunctional work family, shifty spies, old enemies, and new friends who might just be enemies.

The moment he heard the creak of the front porch, Vic Walker knew someone was there to kill him. He had expected it, planned for it. In the fifteen years he'd worked in the business, he'd acquired quite a few enemies—old adversaries who wanted payback, and more than one former friend who might just want to kill him. What irritated Vic was that his attacker was so damned sloppy. Sloppy, and yet the bastard had gotten past his security measures. Knowing it had probably been a mistake and that there was something wrong with his first line of defense just pissed him off.

He waited, lying still on the couch and feigning sleep. Soft steps, only one set of footsteps. Didn't mean the intruder didn't have a partner, but at least only one had breached his security—for the moment. The footsteps sounded light, so Vic was pretty sure his intruder was smaller than average.

Easy pickings.

He held his breath as he waited. The front door opened. The bastard had slipped the dead bolt. A pro for sure, because without the squeak on the porch, Vic would still be asleep.

Soft, steady footsteps drew nearer as his assailant approached the couch. So close now, Vic could feel the heat and smell the night air on his attacker. The figure paused, and Vic sensed he was being studied. Adrenaline rushed through his blood as anticipation danced over his flesh. Patience had never been one of his best virtues in his personal life, but it was another matter on the job. In that one moment, Vic grabbed the attacker's wrist, yanking hard so he landed on top of Vic. With one fluid move, he rolled off the couch and pinned his adversary to the floor. The moment he rolled over the intruder, he knew it wasn't a man. The body was too slight and just a little bit too curvy.

"Bloody hell, Vic."

He knew that smoky voice. It haunted his dreams and drove him to distraction during the day. English tainted the edges just enough to remind him of the time they had spent working in her birth country.

MacKenzie Donovan.

Former British spy, CIA informant, and his ex-partner—not to mention lover.

Ex-lover. He needed to remember the ex part.

Vic leaned up on his elbows and looked down at her. It was still dark in the room, but he had good night vision. Her hair was brown again and fanned out against the worn rug beneath her. Anger and amusement glittered in her green eyes. His heart ached just looking at her.

"What the hell are you doing here?"

"Nice to see you again, lover," she said.

She looked just the way he remembered. That perfect porcelain skin begged for his touch, while the exotic slant of her soft green eyes always fooled a man into thinking she was sweet. Before any adversary discovered the truth, he was left bruised and bloody. Vic knew better and had the physical and emotional scars to prove it.

He'd known when he walked out on their partnership that he wouldn't see her again unless he went looking. Not this time. He had stood his ground and fought the urge to apologize. Six months had passed, and he had refused to give in. Granted, there was still a small part of him that had wanted her to come looking for him.

Now, here she was, the woman he had thought would be the one for him. She lay beneath him, and with each breath, he drew in a bit of her unique scent. Of course, he reacted as he always did when they found themselves in this situation. It took all of his control not to press his growing erection against her and surrender to the need. Hell, he didn't have to. There was no doubt in his mind she felt it, too, as he watched one sculpted eyebrow rise.

"You're frowning at me, but I can tell there are other parts of you that are happy to see me."

Her voice had grown huskier...deeper. Arousal threaded every syllable. Dammit, she was tempting. He had power in every part of his life, except with Mac. She knew which buttons to push, and they always ended up in bed. Angry sex was always her go-to for resolving their differences. Because he wanted to strip them both naked and bury himself inside of her, he made a sound of disgust and released his hold.

He rolled to his feet, ready to defend himself. She might be flirty, but that meant nothing. With Mac, you could never be too sure she wouldn't turn on you. She would kiss you one minute and shoot you the next. It was one of the sexiest things about her.

She raised herself to her elbows and looked at him. The smile she gave him could only be termed as sinister, and dammit, his cock twitched in admiration. He had always had a fast trigger where she was concerned. Even after a six-month separation, he hadn't gotten any better at controlling himself.

"You do know how to live, Vic. Midnight on a Saturday night, and you're in your pj's, sleeping on the couch." She glanced over at the side table where his half-empty whiskey bottle sat next to his glass. "It's not a good sign that you're drinking alone."

He hated that he missed this, the banter, the sparring. They were excellent at it, in fact. Hell, he regretted every second he'd pined for her over the last six months. It had been fun at first. A little fight. A little making up. And always, always, a lot of sex.

Somewhere down the line, it had ended up just being fights and no sex. Making up became impossible. Worse, it had seemed as if she hadn't wanted to make up. When he'd started wondering if she even cared if he were around, he decided it was time to leave.

"Do you want to explain the midnight visit, Mac?"

Her smile dimmed, and she rolled to her feet as efficiently as he had and shoved a hand through her hair. He followed the motion, knowing just how it felt to have those silky strands slip through his fingers. He loved that she kept it long. It was almost down to her waist, and both of them knew it was a stupid decision. Having her hair that length gave her enemy a weapon, but it was the one thing she'd said she would never give up.

"We've got a problem."

It was his turn to raise an eyebrow. He crossed his arms over his chest. "I don't think *we* have a problem. Remember, I signed most everything over to you. You, and whoever is working for you, have a problem."

"You're still an owner on paper, and we have a shit storm of a mess raining down on us in DC."

Concern immediately blossomed. Mac wasn't a woman who exaggerated about work. Most of the time, she pretended as if all hell hadn't broken loose. If she said it was bad, it was probably beyond fixable.

Dammit, he would not be drawn back in. But even as he thought that, he heard himself say, "Explain."

"Not going to offer me a spot of tea?"

He could fight her. It was something they were good at doing. He would order her to tell him, and she would tell him to bugger off. It usually ended up with them in bed.

Instead, he decided to make her tea.

"Come on."

He held his hand out, and she looked offended. He might be in love with the woman, but he didn't trust her. He knew she was still pissed he'd walked away from their business, WD & Associates. With a huff, she handed him her favorite knife. There was a good chance she had more waiting for him, but this was probably the most lethal weapon. Mac knew just how to cut a man to hurt him, not to mention kill him.

He turned on the light on his way to the kitchen. It was small and utilitarian, unlike the efficient gourmet kitchen he had in his Alexandria townhouse. He hadn't come here to cook, but to contemplate his life and his relationship with Mac. The thinking he had planned on doing had stretched out over several months.

As he put the kettle on the burner, she settled at the breakfast bar. She looked like she always did: ready and willing for a fight or a laugh. She dug into her pocket and retrieved a hair band. With economical movements, she pulled her hair up into a sassy tail. The black knit shirt and black jeans were standard issue for Mac, especially when she was breaking and entering.

Those were the things everyone else would see, but Vic could see beneath the surface. She kept glancing around, her gaze darting from one dark corner to the next. Most people would think she was studying the room, but he knew it was a tell for her. She was nervous—and that was a first for them. She had always seemed to have the upper hand. By the time she made eye contact again, there was a sneer on her face.

"Nice place, Vic. Real early American. Do you have indoor plumbing?"

Even when she joked, it was easy to hear the edge in her voice and see the telltale tremor in her fingers. Most people wouldn't notice it, but he knew Mac better than he knew himself. She was definitely in trouble.

"So, explain."

She hesitated. The woman had come to him for help, and she still didn't want to tell him what was going on. Nothing much ever changed. She was always running from a bad situation and lying to him.

"I took on a job a few weeks ago. Surveillance. And it wasn't much of anything, until everything went wrong."

Of course. "What happened?"

"We were watching this Englishman, a diplomat's son. The NSA thinks he might be selling secrets to support his whore habit."

He bit back a growl. The main reason they had dissolved the partnership was due to Mac's insistence on working with government agencies. Vic had thought it was a good idea at first, until every job they had with the NSA had gone to hell.

The government could be notoriously late with their payments, too.

"Not an uncommon tale. Why didn't they have the FBI look into it?"

She rolled her eyes. "They wanted to turn him. If they sent the FBI in, they could have lost the chance at gaining an asset. Someone like him, he could have fed all kinds of info back to them. Seems Michael doesn't give a damn about anyone but himself, and the NSA was pretty sure they could entice him over to their side with a little blackmail and some money. Truth is, Michael doesn't care where the money comes from, just that he has enough of it. Add in the red tape in getting one agency to work for another agency—because who wants to deal with Congress? The NSA wanted someone who would disappear when the job was done."

"Nothing new," he said, as the teakettle started to whistle. He poured water into the two mugs and handed her one. She took hold of the string and gave it a look of disgust.

"Really, after all these years, you still can't make a decent mug of tea. Don't you keep any good tea leaves on hand?"

He ignored her and waited. One thing about Mac was that she needed to bitch about small things while she led up to the clusterfuck she wanted to drop in his lap.

"So, the kid—"

"Michael?"

She nodded. "Michael Wyndham. He's got something going on. We pick up talk of a package, but we've no idea what it is. Worse, he shows up one night with a woman, but this one is kind of young—and not the usual kind of woman for him."

Vic turned cold. "How young?"

She sighed. "Legal, that's for sure, but Rock knew from the look of her that she was in way over her head."

Rock would. Bryan Rocovich was Vic's best friend and could be counted on in any situation.

"Go on."

"Rock was pretty sure there was more to it than just a tumble in bed. Worse, she was acting weird, as if she had been drugged."

"The bastard."

She nodded.

"How do we get from an innocent being drugged to you creeping onto my property?"

"Well, you know Rock. Since he lost Annabelle, he can't stand watching a woman being hurt, so he blew the operation and stole the girl."

He stopped drinking and stared at her. "What do you mean 'he blew the operation?'"

"I mean he walked into the bastard's flat and knocked him out cold. He took the girl and headed out the door. But not before he ran into the Russians who had ordered her. *She* was the package. By the time he made it back to headquarters, the girl was awake and asking questions, and there were three dead Russians, a bleeding son of a diplomat, and a Russian crime boss after us. Worse, they have connections. The FBI showed up at the office door, but we were already out the back."

Fubar did not even begin to cover it. In all the years they had worked together, he could not remember anything exploding like this, but he had warned of it. Government agencies could not be trusted, especially the NSA. He trusted them less than the CIA, and that was saying a lot. "Where's the girl?"

Mac hesitated. Irritation and worry dug deep into his gut. A bad sign. She was up front about work, but when she avoided telling him things, it always turned out to be worse than he imagined.

"Spit it out, Mac."

"She's with Jay."

For a second, he just stared at her, wondering when Mac had slipped over the edge. She had always played on that edge, balancing on it like a fucking prima ballerina, but this was beyond anything he had thought she would do.

"You thought leaving a scared young woman with my brother was a good idea?" he yelled.

She winced, and he immediately regretted it.

He didn't apologize, though. She would see it as a weakness. "Did you make sure you weren't followed here?"

"What do you take me for?"

Indeed. If there was one woman who knew how to take care of herself, it was MacKenzie Donovan. She had told him that much when she'd told him to go to hell when he left.

"And, you're here, why?"

"I came to warn you. I tried to get Jay to let me take her, but he seems to think it's best she stays with him. As of right now, he's not on the payroll. It appears that way, at least, so he is probably right."

"I don't know why you just didn't..." he trailed off, realizing what she had just said. "Don't tell me you hired my brother."

There was another long pause, and she looked everywhere but at him. "Okay, I didn't."

He let the ramifications settle between them. "What the hell, Mac? Just what the bloody hell? You leave a woman with him, a woman you say is innocent in all this, but how do we know? She could be dangerous, and Jay won't know what hit him."

"Seriously, she's innocent. She was drugged, and when she was coming out of it, she freaked the hell out. And I had to hire your brother. There aren't a lot of men I can have on the team that I can trust. Since you abandoned me, I needed to come up with other means to run the operation."

He decided to let that comment go. "So you decided to hire my brother and leave an innocent with him? Are you out of your bleeding mind? He sleeps with anything pretty."

"She's not his type."

"Does he have a type? I'm pretty sure that my brother has slept with women of every skin color, nationality, and religious background."

"Your brother has two types of women he will not sleep with. One, me—but the feeling is mutual. Then, there are virgins." She sighed. "She's either a virgin or damned near close."

He blew out a breath, some of his worry dissolving. "Okay, not my brother's type."

"So she's with him, Rock is on his way to the safe house, and I came here. It's a good thing I am good at losing any kind of tail, because you have some pretty shoddy security."

"It isn't shoddy."

The smile she leveled in his direction was filled with snark. Damn if that didn't go straight to his gut—not to mention his cock.

"I got through."

"That doesn't mean anything. You could probably break into the Pentagon."

Her expression softened. There was no other woman he knew who would go soft when accused of being good at breaking and entering. Just knowing that and seeing her reaction softened his heart. How did she get to him so easily?

"Thank you, but it is shoddy. Seriously, you need some earlier alarms."

The moment she said it, his skin prickled. It was the sign something was about to go very, very wrong. He stilled, waiting. He could feel the energy zap in the air.

"What?" she asked.

He shook his head, killing the light as he made his way to the window. He wished he had his night-vision goggles, but even without them, Vic knew. No animals. No noise.

Fuck.

He was already heading to his bedroom when the first alarm sounded. After stripping out of his flannel pj bottoms, he tugged on a pair of jeans and grabbed a shirt.

"Dammit to hell," Mac said. She reached behind her and pulled a gun from her waistband, following him into his room. "I know I didn't have a tail."

"Well, one way or another, they found us. We need to get the hell out of here."

He opened his closet and then the hidden panel where he kept his weapons. He pulled two M16s out and threw one to Mac. She caught it with a smile and stuck her Glock in her waistband again.

"Nice." Even with the situation they were in, he caught the arousal in her voice. The woman had a hard-on for anything that could maim or kill.

Another alarm sounded.

"How much time?" she asked.

He turned in the direction of the garage. "Five minutes at most."

She followed him without question. Mac was still mad at him, she was still pissed about the way he'd left her and the company, but she knew not to fuck around in a situation like this. She knew when to argue and when to follow orders. He threw his go bag in the backseat of the pickup and grabbed another bag of ammo. Mac was already in the passenger seat.

The second alarm went off, and Vic knew they had less than two minutes to get their asses out of there. He could have used the bunker to hide in, but there was a good chance that if these were the Russians after Mac, they would find it.

He started up the engine of his truck and hit the remote for the garage door. He went out behind the house, making it easier to escape anyone coming up the front. As he gunned the engine, he heard shots behind him, but paid no attention. They were still too far off to even hit the truck. Vic didn't want to try firing back. It was better just to lose them and get somewhere safe. Maybe then they could figure this all out.

Of course, Mac did the exact opposite. She opened the window, slipped up to the edge of the car door, and started shooting.

"Mac, get your ass back in here."

She ignored him. After she fired a few shots behind them, she easily slid back into the cab of the pickup.

"Do you ever listen?" he demanded.

"When the advice isn't rubbish, I listen."

He wanted to argue with her. Hell, he wanted to demand she listen to him and only him. He'd lost the right to that and so much more when he walked out of their office—and out of her life—months ago. It was the only thing he could do to keep himself sane.

But his life never worked out the way he wanted it to. No matter how many plans he made, he always seemed to end up back at square one, fighting his way out. This time, though, he had his head on straight. Time away from her, away from the job, had left him with enough control that he could look at the situation rationally. All he had to do was figure out the mess they were all in and clean it up. And he had to do it before he got pulled back into the craziness of Mac and her life. He knew this time he wouldn't survive if he went under for a third time.

acknowledgments

I know I say this with every book, but there is no book that is written without the help of a lot of people in the background.

First, a big thank you to my cover artist Scott Carpenter. We have been working together for over twenty years and you always amaze me with what you do for my work.

A big thanks to Noel Varner for helping me get this book into shape.

Thanks to Brandy Walker for always keeping my spirits up while I trudge through deadlines.

And finally, to my family, Les and the girls, for helping me while I fought off several colds this summer. You are the best.

about the author

From an early age, USA Today Best-selling author Melissa loved to read. When she discovered the romance genre, she started to listen to the voices in her head. After years of following her AF Major husband around, she is happy to be settled in Northern Virginia surrounded by horses, wineries, and many, many Wegmans.

Keep up with Mel, her releases, and her appearances by subscribing to her <u>NEWSLETTER</u>. If you want to keep up with cover reveals, new behind the scene info on her writing, and when new excerpts are posted, follow her MelissaSchroeder.net News . Or you can do both! They are low traffic, so you will not get tons of emails.

If you want to check out Mel's writing soundtracks, they are posted on her website on the individual book pages.

Check out all her other books, family trees and other info at
<u>her website!</u>
<u>If you would want contact Mel, email her at: melissa@</u>
<u>melissaschroeder.net</u>

www.ingramcontent.com/pod-product-compliance
Lightning Source LLC
Chambersburg PA
CBHW020103180626
46812CB00006B/2448